# Joe Tries to Catch a Murderer

*By B. Heather Mantler*

I dedicate this book to the teachers at Okanagan College, who made this book so fun to write though they did not know it at the time. Also dedicated to Jenna Tulak, who did know and contributed the poem Ten Thousand Footprints in the Sand and a couple names I had forgotten.

# Chapter One
## The Body

Shawn 'Shorty' Jennings kicked the dust off his boots before stepping up on to Mrs. Grady's porch. He was just about to take his hat off before knocking, but a scraping sound from inside made him stop. Shorty listened for any further sounds. When he did not hear any he removed his hat. He reached out to knock and stopped again. Giggling came from inside. Shorty stood there frozen and the giggling continued. It was coming from the main floor and this side of the house. Shorty slowly moved to the window. He peeked inside.

There was Mrs. Grady sitting on the settee and giggling. Sitting beside her and kissing her in improper places, was Slick McQueen. Slick was known for his gang of thugs who did what they pleased and shot at anyone who argued. But Mrs. Grady was not arguing and Len Grady was not due back until tomorrow.

Shorty moved back from the window as quietly as he could. He placed his hat back on his head as he moved off the porch. Shorty glanced around to make sure none of Slick's gang was in sight. He did not see anyone. Shorty glanced back at the house, but no one inside was interested in what was happening outside. Shorty sped up as he headed down the lane to where he had hitched up his horse. His reason for being there long forgotten.

"Are you sure about taking him?" the deputy asked as he watched Sheriff Broddy saddle the second horse the deputy usually rode.

"Laws are laws," Sheriff Broddy answered, "There is a body and the law says two men have to go check it out."

"But the saloon owner?" the deputy asked, "I'm not sure he is trustworthy enough."

"He is trustworthy," Sheriff Broddy answered, "He is the only in town who I am sure will never tell anyone else. He is also the only member of the town council available at this time of day."

"I am sure Mr. Henczel would be willing to go out with you," the deputy said.

"And report it in the paper immediately after," Sheriff Broddy said, "I don't know what happened yet and I certainly am not ready to publish it in the paper."

"Doc McKaig shouldn't be too long," the deputy said, "You can wait for him."

"Mr. McGraw is fully capable of accompanying me on this errand," Sheriff Broddy said, "Whether you find him agreeable or not."

"He plays at being agreeable," the deputy said, "I don't trust him."

"Hold down the fort," Sheriff Broddy said as he mounted his horse while keeping the reins from the other horse in his hand, "I might be a while."

"Be careful," the deputy said as Sheriff Broddy rode passed him.


Joe McGraw sat at the end of the bar looking over the rest of the saloon. He had a shot of whisky near him on the bar and a cigar in his hand. It was just past two in the afternoon and aside from Jake Kennedy, the bartender, the place was empty. Joe was okay with that as he took a drag from his cigar and thought about the sunshine coming in through dust covered windows. Jake was busy cleaning and organizing stuff behind the bar, so everything would be ready when people started coming in for the evening.

Joe smiled slightly to himself. It was going to be a busy night and he was going to enjoy it from his spot here at the bar. Everyone in town knew where to find him. They also knew his saloon was the place to go when they had money they needed to spend. And since there wasn't another saloon for a couple towns in any direction this was the place people spent it.

The swinging door was pushed open and Sheriff Broddy stepped inside. He didn't even bother to glance around, just headed straight for Joe's chair and letting the door swing behind him.

"What can I do for you, Sheriff?" Joe asked before taking another puff from his cigar.

"You're the only town councillor available," Sheriff Broddy answered, "And I need one out at the Grady place now."

"What happened?" Joe asked as he put out his cigar in the ash tray on the bar.

"Better to tell you on the way," Sheriff Broody answered.

"Be right down," Joe said as he stood up. Sheriff Broddy crossed his arms over his chest and waited. Joe headed up the red velvet stairs to the second floor.

Joe carefully pulled on his jacket, adjusted his sleeves, and then made sure it was lint free. He checked himself in the mirror before placing his hat on perfectly styled hair. Only once he was sure his outfit was right did Joe head back down stairs.

Sheriff Broddy looked Joe over as he came down the stairs and shook his head.

"Open as usual if I'm not back in time," Joe told Jake as he passed the bar.

"Yes, sir," Jake said with a nod.

"Let's go then," Joe said waving the sheriff toward the door.

Sheriff Broddy turned on his heel and walked out of the saloon. Joe followed.

Outside there were two horses tied to the hitching post. One was Sheriff Broddy's mustang and the other was the deputy's chestnut nag.

"We don't have time for you to saddle your own," Sheriff Broddy said as he mounted his horse, "And my deputy is needed here in my absence anyway."

"So, what is this emergency?" Joe asked as he mounted the nag. He would have liked to ride his own stallion, but was not going to try and make Sheriff Broddy wait. Sheriff Broddy did not answer immediately as they started down the main street to the end of town.

It was not a long street, but it was the only one in town. The saloon had gotten a prime spot at its middle. Across from it was the general store run by Carrie Gilbert and her husband. From there the other businesses radiated outward with the sheriff's office and jail half-way up from the saloon. The business owners had their houses behind their businesses and the rest came from their ranches when they needed something. A coach passed through about twice a week, but the Lanaway Hotel had limited rooms. Joe only rented his rooms out to the women who worked the saloon and Sheriff Broddy was known to have his say over who could stay in town.

"We got a death out there at the Grady place," Sheriff Broddy answered once they were passed the stable and the blacksmith's shop into the open country.

"Len ain't due back until tomorrow," Joe said.

"Apparently he came home early," Sheriff Broddy said, "Because I can't see anyone willing to drag his body back to dump it on his front porch."

"Shouldn't we be bringing the doc along?" Joe asked.

"I left a message for Doc McKaig to join us as soon as he is finished his lunch," Sheriff Broddy answered, "Until then it's just us."

"And what are we supposed to do?" Joe asked.

"Make sure it ain't a murder and make sure he gets a proper burial," Sheriff Broddy answered.

"And it takes two of us to do that?" Joe asked.

"A requirement written into the civic law when Mr. Brecklin settled the town," Sheriff Broddy answered.

"Kurt was always putting strange laws into place," Joe said, "Don't mean we follow them all."

"They're followed," Sheriff Broddy said. Joe shook his head but did not argue. Sheriff Broddy seemed fine with that since he did not bother to add more conversation. Instead they rode without talking.

Joe had never been to the Grady place, but he knew where it was. The lane into the place was fairly long with the house at the end. The land was all fenced in to keep the dozen or so of Grady's herd from wandering into someone else's herd. At the end of the lane was the house. It was two storey with a porch along the front. The door was in the middle of the porch with a window on each side. There was a garden visible behind the house, but the yard was just the same dirt as the lane.

As Sheriff Broddy and Joe got closer to the house, Joe could see the body lying on the porch with one foot sticking out over the stairs. There was no one else around.

"Who let you know about Len?" Joe asked.

"Anders stopped by," Sheriff Broddy answered, "Said he was checking on Len's herd."

"Why would Anders be checking on Len's herd?" Joe asked, "Len doesn't like Anders on his property."

"I asked Anders that same question," Sheriff Broddy said, "He said the people Len usually asks are all out of town. He said I could ask Myra Grady if I wanted and she could confirm his story."

"Have you found Mrs. Grady to confirm his story?" Joe asked.

"Not yet," Sheriff Broddy answered, "I'm hoping she is over at Laine's place."

"I guess we are about to find out," Joe said as they stopped their horses. After getting down, they tied the reins around the hitching post and walked over to the body. It was definitely Len Grady and if the knife in his chest was any indication his death was not natural.

"Damn," Sheriff Broddy muttered.

"Looks like you are going to investigate a murder," Joe said.

"Damn," Sheriff Broddy said.

Joe was about to move forward when he looked down and noticed two sets of fresh footprints in the dirt. Both were the size of men's boots. One pair had a v marked in the bottom. Joe was careful not to scuff the boot prints as he moved closer to the body. The body had not been there long as the blood was still dripping through the boards of the porch and into the dirt below.

"That is Len's knife," Sheriff Broddy said from the other side of the stairs as he was also being careful of the boot prints.

"Len was never the fastest man around," Joe commented.

"Even then it takes something to walk up to someone and grab their own knife," Sheriff Broddy said, "Takes guts to do that."

"Probably the same amount to use the knife to stab the person," Joe said.

"You're probably right," Sheriff Broddy said.

"Is there a back door?" Joe asked.

"Only times I've been out here I have stayed out front," Sheriff Broddy answered.

Joe was careful about stepping back from the porch.

"What are you doing?" Sheriff Broddy asked.

"I thought I would check the house," Joe answered.

"Are you expecting the murderer to be caught inside?" Sheriff Broddy asked.

"Nope," Joe answered.

"Don't get lost," Sheriff Broddy said.

Joe walked around the house. There were no more fresh boot prints, but it did appear that a horse had been through recently. Behind the house was a stable for horses with its door hanging open. Joe could not see inside but he could not hear any animals. There was a back door. Joe went up the steps and pulled open the door.

He stepped into the kitchen and closed the door behind him. There were a couple tea cups sitting on the table with a tea pot. Joe touched the side of the tea pot and found it room temperature. He moved into the hallway, which went straight through to the front door with the doorways off it and the stairs heading up to the second floor. Joe went through the doorway on the right and found himself in the sitting room. It was well furnished with a settee and a couple chairs. The floor was hardwood and the walls were varnished panelling. Outside the large window, Joe could see the sheriff studying the body.

Joe turned to leave the room when something shiny caught his eye. It was just under the edge of the settee. He went over and crouched down to examine it. The object was the stud off a man's pants. Len would never have worn such pants because they were hardly practical for ranching. It would more likely come from someone who did not do physical work. Also the body lying on the porch was wearing jeans. Joe picked it up and put it in his pocket.

The rest of the house contained nothing of interest. The room on the other side had been the dining room. Upstairs was the master bedroom and a guest room. It did not appear that anyone had been up there since the bed had been turned down. Joe left the house through the kitchen door before going around to the front. The sheriff had sat down on swing on the porch.

"Anything?" Sheriff Broddy asked.

"Just this," Joe answered taking the stud out of his pocket. Sheriff Broddy peered at it for a moment.

"Ain't his," Sheriff Broddy said pointing to the body.

"I didn't think so," Joe said. He leaned against the porch railing. Neither man spoke for several minutes.

"How long was doc going to be?" Joe asked.

"In a rush to be somewhere?" Sheriff Broddy asked.

"Yeah," Joe answered, "The sooner I'm out of the sun the happier I am."

"He said he would be right along after he finished lunch," Sheriff Broddy said, "He was just starting when I left him in his kitchen. Shouldn't be too much longer."

"I don't remember anybody having troubles with Len," Joe said.

"Not many did," Sheriff Broddy said, "Len had more trouble with Anders than Anders had with him. Considering Anders's tendency to acquire cattle, the ranchers have troubles with him."

"Any troubles between them lately?" Joe asked.

"Not I've been told," Sheriff Broddy answered, "No one has told me of troubles with Anders lately."

"Maybe he feels his herd is big enough," Joe said.

Broddy snorted with suppressed laughter.

Joe looked down the road and saw a horse coming towards them.

"Looks like Doc McKaig is on his way," Joe said.

Broddy looked up.

"Looks like," Sheriff Broddy said.

They watched the horse come closer until they could see that is was actually pulling a wagon with Doc Kaig sitting in the driver's seat. He pulled up beside the porch and then stopped the horse.

"Hello, boys," Doc McKaig tipped his hat to them.

"Hello, Doc," Sheriff Broddy said.

Doc McKaig moved his bulk to the edge and then stepped

down. He went over to the body and studied it for several moments.

"Definitely dead," Doc McKaig said.

"You sure?" Broddy asked.

Doc McKaig looked up at the sheriff.

"Hard to live with a knife that deep in the heart," Doc McKaig said, "But I suppose it is possible. Has he sat up to tell you he ain't dead?"

"Nope," Broddy answered.

"Then he's dead," Doc McKaig said, "Help me get him into the wagon."

The sheriff got to his feet, but Joe was much slower to move.

"I didn't peg you as the squeamish sort, boy," Doc McKaig said.

"He ain't," Broddy said, "Joe just doesn't like to get dirty."

"Blood is hard enough to get out of clothing the piece might as well be burned," Joe said.

"Then you get the feet," Doc McKaig said, "Dust is easier to brush off."

Doc McKaig and the sheriff took the arms while Joe took Len's feet. He frowned when the dirty boots touched his suit, but there was little he could do about it. They moved the body from the porch into the wagon. Joe let go as soon as he could. While Doc McKaig was putting a tarp over the body, Joe worked to get every speck of dust of his clothes.

"Where's Len's wife?" Doc McKaig asked.

"I believe she is at Laine's," Sheriff Broddy answered, "I was going to head over there after this."

"She needs to come around and tell me where she wants him buried," Doc McKaig said.

"I will tell her," Sheriff Broddy said.

Doc McKaig heaved himself up on to the driver's seat of the wagon. He clicked his tongue to get his horse moving. Sheriff Broddy went to study the place where the body had been, but there was nothing left except the blood stain.

"Is it telling you anything?" Joe asked.

"Nope," Sheriff Broddy answered, "But I keep hoping."

Sheriff Broddy went off to the horses and Joe followed.

"Laine's place is on the way to town," Sheriff Broddy said.

"Yes, it is," Joe said with a sigh.

They mounted the horses and started back down the road. There was no conversation as they went.

Laine's place was on ranch land out of town. There was very little land around the building. The building itself was one storey but stretched out as if there were two wings. The wood had not been treated and there was no glass in the windows just shutters.

The sheriff and Joe stopped at the hitching post, where they left the horses before going to the door. The door opened before they actually reached it. Amy Modhal stood there.

"Good afternoon, Sheriff, Mr. McGraw," Miss. Modhal said, "What brings you out all this way?"

"We are looking for Mrs. Grady," Sheriff Broddy said.

"She was here earlier this week," Miss. Modhal said, "But she left yesterday evening and hasn't been back."

"Are you sure?" Sheriff Broddy asked, "Because we didn't find her at home."

"She said she wanted to be home when Len arrived," Miss. Modhal answered, "But you can ask Miss. Laine, if you want."

"No, it is all right," Sheriff Broddy said, "I believe you. If she does show up here, let her know I am looking for her."

"I will," Miss. Modhal said.

"Thank you," Sheriff Broddy said with a tip of his hat. She smiled in return.

The sheriff and Joe returned to the hitching post. They mounted and started back toward town. Miss. Modhal watched them for a moment more before going back inside and closing the door.

"Could she be in town?" Sheriff Broddy asked.

"She and Gillian Jarratt are friends," Joe answered, "But I'm not sure who else she would visit. I have never paid much attention to her behaviour as it was Len who would come in for a drink."

"Then why do you know she is friends with Mrs. Jarratt?" Sheriff Broddy asked.

"Where do you think she went while he came in for a drink?" Joe replied.

The sheriff nodded.

They rode through to the sheriff's office and around to the stable at the back. After unsaddling the horses and putting them away in the stalls, Joe followed the sheriff out of the stable. They headed for the tailoring shop.

Entering the shop, they found Mrs. Jarratt pinning the hem of a dress. She glanced up at them before going back to her work.

"Can I help you with something, sheriff?" Mr. Jarratt asked stepping out from behind the screen that separated the front of the shop with the back.

"I was wondering if you have heard or seen Mrs. Grady today," Sheriff Broddy said.

"Not today," Mr. Jarratt said.

"She is at home," Mrs. Jarratt said, "Because her husband gets home today. If she isn't there, she may still be at Laine's place."

"Looked at both," Sheriff Broddy said, "And she wasn't either place. If you see her, let her know I need to talk to her."

"Certainly, Sheriff," Mr. Jarratt said.

"Why?" Mrs. Jarratt stopped her work to look at the sheriff. She glanced at Joe briefly before looking at the sheriff again.

"Because Len Grady isn't going to be home again," Sheriff Broddy answered.

Mrs. Jarratt nodded but didn't say anything more. Joe followed Sheriff Broddy as he left the shop.

"Anywhere else?" Joe asked as they stood on the sidewalk. The stagecoach was coming into town.

"I can't think of anywhere else," Sheriff Broddy answered as his eyes followed the stagecoach, "I'll send my deputy out to the Grady place to keep an eye out for her."

"Then I will go back to my business," Joe said.

Sheriff Broddy nodded.

Joe headed down the sidewalk towards his saloon. He kept an eye on the stagecoach as he went. It stopped in front of the hotel, which was on the opposite side of the street so Joe could not see the people who got off. By the time Joe reached the doors to his saloon, the stagecoach was being moved around back to exchange horses. All passengers had gone into the hotel.

It was darker inside the saloon, so it took a moment before Joe could see clearly. It was no longer just Jake; a couple men stood at the bar and the game had been started at the back. Dewihite was sitting in his usual place at the game with Shorty Johnston behind him and Miss. Karina on his arm. Miss Karina gave Joe a seductive smile, but Joe was smart enough to not mess with someone else's woman.

Joe went to his place at the end of the bar and sat down. Everything was as he left it. He relit the cigar and took a long inhale. The man closest moved even closer. Joe looked over to see that is was McPherson, the editor of the town newspaper.

"What do you want?" Joe asked.

"What did the sheriff want you for?" McPherson asked, "Which of Brecklin's laws did he have to enact?"

"What does it matter?" Joe asked.

"It has been months since Broddy demanded the presence of a town councillor," McPherson said, "And he's never asked you to help with those matters. So, what matter would he ask for your help and not anyone else?"

"Sheriff Broddy said there was no one else available," Joe

said.

"Ed has been sitting out by the sheriff's office all day," McPherson said.

"Would you take Henczel anywhere?" Joe asked, "Especially on days when he has been sitting out by the sheriff's office?"

"Ed knows Brecklin's laws better than anyone in town," McPherson said.

"Then we should make him mayor at the next election," Joe said.

"He may exhibit curious behaviour, but he has never been ambitious," McPherson said.

"You mean he would rather be an advisor rather than a figure head," Joe said.

"You could run for mayor," McPherson said.

"I have a business to run," Joe said, "I don't need the headaches related to trying to run a town."

"So, what did the sheriff need of you?" McPherson asked.

"Why aren't you at his office badgering him?" Joe asked.

"Maybe I will later," McPherson said, "But since I am here, why aren't you willing to tell me what is going on?"

"Because it isn't my story to tell," Joe said.

"You never tell any of your stories, so I am more likely to get you to tell other people's," McPherson said.

"Not this time," Joe said.

The doors to the saloon opened and a woman with a suitcase stepped inside. She was in a green satin dress with black lace trim and a hat to match. Her brown hair had a shine despite most of it hiding beneath the hat. Her hazel eyes glanced around the room as they were adjusting to the dark. Finally those eyes settled on Joe and she walked over.

McPherson glanced behind him when Joe didn't respond to his latest question.

"Wow," McPherson said under his breath.

"Mr. McGraw?" the voice had the same smoothness

suggested by her dress.

"I am," Joe answered.

"Mr. Lanaway from the hotel suggested I come over here," the woman said, "The rooms at the hotel are full and I am in need of a room for a few days."

McPherson glanced at Joe, knowing full well what type of woman Joe let use the rooms. The woman obviously did not know.

"I can pay," the woman said when Joe didn't immediately answer.

"I suppose," Joe answered, "As long as it is only for a few days."

"Thank you," the woman said with a smile.

Joe nodded before getting to his feet. He went behind the bar to get a key to an upstairs room. Then he stepped back out from behind the bar.

"This way," Joe said before leading the way up the stairs. She followed with her suitcase in her hand. At the top of the stairs, Joe went down the hallway to the room just before his own suite. He unlocked the door and held it open. The woman stepped inside and looked around.

The room had a large bed with a cloth canopy. There was a soft covered chair and a dresser. The window had a sheer curtain keeping people from seeing inside while letting in the sunlight.

"Thank you, Mr. McGraw," the woman smiled at Joe again, "I really appreciate you letting me stay."

"Joe."

"Scarlett." She held out her gloved hand. Joe shook it before offering her the key. She took it.

"Enjoy your stay," Joe said.

"I think I will," Scarlett said with a seductive smile.

Joe left her to settle in and went back down to his place at the bar. McPherson was still sitting there.

"I thought you were going to go talk to the sheriff," Joe

said before taking a sip of his whiskey.

"After you let such a lady stay here?" McPherson asked, "In rooms you don't rent out, except to certain type of ladies."

"I doubt she is that type of lady," Joe said, "Despite her asking to stay here. Lanaway is full and she has nowhere else to stay. Laine's place is quite a walk from here. Besides you never partake of the women who stay here because you have your fiancée out east."

"And I will continue not to partake in anything with any woman staying here," McPherson said, "But for the first time since I have met you, you looked stunned. I didn't think it was possible for you to be brought down to the level of the rest of us mortal men."

"I am as human as everyone else," Joe said, "And I have had plenty of troubles with women. I have also learned plenty from those troubles."

"So, she didn't get under your skin?" McPherson asked, "Because it sure looked like she did."

"I didn't say she didn't," Joe said, "I just said I have learned from previous experiences with women."

"Tell me more," McPherson said.

"No," Joe said.

"You won't tell me other people's stories," McPherson said, "And you won't tell me your stories. I need something to print in my newspaper."

"How about you find someone else to write about?" Joe asked.

"What fun is that?" McPherson asked.

Joe gave McPherson a go-away look. McPherson took his drink and moved back down the bar. Joe picked up his cigar and took an inhale off it. As McPherson implied, Joe found his mind stuck on Scarlett.

Sheriff Broddy poured himself another cup of coffee. He took it back to his desk and sat down. Leaning back,

Sheriff Broddy looked out the window. He could see the side of Henczel's head in the disappearing light outside the office. Sheriff Broddy thought about lighting a lamp, but he was not ready to do that yet. He knew Henczel would go home shortly and if he knew Sheriff Broddy was inside the office he would likely come in and asked what caused Sheriff Broddy to head out of town.

As much as he understood people wanting to know about deaths, Sheriff Broddy was not ready to advertise a murder had happened. It would make the investigation harder. Sheriff Broddy took a sip of coffee. He wondered who would want to kill Len Grady. It did not make sense. No one benefited from his death.

"Good evening," the deputy's voice came from outside.

"Good evening," Henczel replied, "When is the sheriff due in?"

"He is probably off having supper," the deputy replied, "You might be better off coming back later tonight."

"Maybe that is what I will do," Henczel said. Sheriff Broddy saw him get up and then leave. The door opened and the deputy stepped inside. He lit the lamp before he noticed Sheriff Broddy seated at the desk.

"He has been moved along," the deputy said.

"I heard," Sheriff Broddy said, "Have you seen Mrs. Grady recently?"

"No, can't say that I have," the deputy answered, "Why?"

"She appears to be missing," Sheriff Broddy answered.

"You want me to conduct a search?" the deputy asked.

"I did some searching earlier," Sheriff Broddy answered, "Just keep an eye out."

"The stagecoach came in," the deputy said.

"I saw," Sheriff Broddy said, "Most will be on their way in the morning. Only one appeared to be trouble and I'm not sure she will be leaving with the rest of them."

"Why not?" the deputy asked.

"Because she looked like trouble," Sheriff Broddy answered.

"You can suggest that she should move along."

"I could but I think I will see how things happen. The Lanaway Hotel is full tonight and she had to seek a room from McGraw."

"He doesn't let anyone stay there."

"She hasn't come out yet, so he must have made an exception for her. That is why I am interesting to see how things play out."

"You think he knows her?"

"I don't know. Depending on how long she stays, we will find out more. Are you off to do your patrol?"

"I thought I would give you some time to eat supper before I went on patrol."

"Head out on patrol."

The deputy nodded before getting a rifle from the rack and heading out. Sheriff Broddy took another sip of coffee but his thoughts were already going back to figuring out a murder.

As he thought it would be, Joe found the evening busy. Those who had taken their cattle to the train station along with Len Grady were also back and had money to spend. Several times Joe ended up helping Jake behind the bar. Miss. Edwards helped out by taking up the role as barmaid. Joe made a mental note to add some to her pay as he usually did when she helped out in addition to her cleaning and cooking.

It was getting later into the night and Joe had managed to reclaim his spot at the end of the bar. Miss. Edwards had retired to her space in the ktichen out back. Jake was starting to clean things up without stopping people from buying more to drink. Scarlett came over from wherever she had been enjoying her evening. Joe had noticed when she had come downstairs. She had left her coat, hat, and gloves upstairs.

Also she was nursing the drink she had bought.

Scarlett sat down on the stool closest to Joe. She set her drink down on the bar. It was down to the last couple mouthfuls, but she did not seem interested in having more added to it. She leaned on arm against the bar as she turned to him.

"Based on what I saw coming into town this afternoon, I would not have thought this many people lived here," Scarlett said.

"You're in ranchland," Joe said, "Many of the places of residence are not along the road."

"Is your residence out of sight out back?" Scarlett asked.

"No," Joe answered, "There is no place out back."

"And yours?" Scarlett asked.

"You are sitting in it," Joe answered.

"And you sleep in one of the rooms upstairs," Scarlett said.

"Usually," Joe said.

"Only usually?" Scarlett asked, "What about those unusual times?"

"I don't sleep those nights," Joe answered, "For a variety of reasons."

"Your wife keeps you wake?" Scarlett asked.

"Does your husband?" Joe replied.

"If you were married to me, would you let me travel by myself?" Scarlett asked.

"Not if I wanted to keep you," Joe answered.

Scarlett lips gave Joe the one sided smiled that suggested he gave the right answer. Joe knew his lips gave an answering smile, but it was more reaction than intention. Her smile got slightly bigger knowing her effect on him.

"Where are you headed?" Joe asked.

"West," Scarlett answered, "I haven't settled on where exactly I want to go. I just didn't want to stay where I was as I was feeling oppressed."

"Feeling freer since you left?" Joe asked.

"Every mile farther away the less I feel it," Scarlett answered, "Don't you ever feel oppressed at times?"

"I like my business," Joe said, "And it provides me with all the freedom I need."

"I have never found ownership to be freeing," Scarlett said, "But I suppose it would be."

"When one is ready it is," Joe said, "But only when the person has found a place they no longer feel oppressed."

"Maybe I will get to such a place someday," Scarlett said.

Matt and Michael started shouting at each other as they slammed down their beers. Matt was the first to stand up and push back his chair. He launched himself across the table at Michael and knocked Michael to the floor damaging the chair in the process. Then the two men rolled around on the floor as they attempted to punch each other.

Everyone else in the saloon started to cheer at the entertainment as they were drunk enough to find it fun. Jake glanced at Joe but got no signal to put an end to the matter, so he went back to serving drinks. Scarlett had turned to watch at the first shout and now looked at Joe again.

"You aren't going to stop it?" Scarlett asked.

"Not yet," Joe answered, "Let them have their fun for a few more minutes."

"Fun?" Scarlett asked.

"Those two like to argue and get into fist fights," Joe answered, "Breaking it up too early just means more gets broken later."

The two men got close to another table and the man closest kicked them away. They went back toward the broken chair.

"Why do you let it happen at all?" Scarlett asked.

"People are here for entertainment," Joe answered.

Scarlett frowned but found herself turning back to watch the two men rolling around on the floor. Those at the tables around kept the fighters in the same area. The players at the game had already turned back to their game as the fight did not hold their attention when there was money on the line. Shorty's laughter could be heard as he continued to watch the fight.

Michael managed to land a punch and several people cheered. Then Matt tried to get one back but he couldn't get his hand free. Instead he slammed Michael's head into the floor. It stunned Michael for long enough for Matt to get his hand free. Rather try to punch Michael, Matt reached out to grab at a piece of broken chair. At that point, Joe got up off his stool. He grabbed the pieces of the broken chair before Matt could find them by feel. Joe put the pieces behind the bar before sitting back down.

The crowd focused on the fight without any comment on Joe's actions. Matt must have seen it out of the corner of his eye because switched from searching to hitting Michael. He had trouble getting enough of a swing to really punch Michael. When it didn't seem to be working, Matt smacked his forehead into Michael's nose. This caused Michael to break from the grapple to hold his nose, but when it didn't immediately start to bleed Michael swung at Matt. Matt swung back. They both had power behind their punches this time. Now both would have black eyes in the morning.

They grappled again and went back to rolling around. The crowded had cheered at the punches thrown and were waiting to see if there were any more good blows. Scarlett managed to turn away from the violence. Instead of turning to Joe, she faced her drink. She finished it in one gulp. Scarlett made that little grimace people give when they down a mouthful of alcohol. Joe was sure it was meant to suggest to him that she wasn't much of a drinker, but he was sure she drank often enough to avoid doing it.

"I think it might be the best time for me to turn in for the night," Scarlett said as she stood up.

"Good night," Joe said.

"Good night," Scarlett said before sweeping passed him and up the stairs. Joe didn't watch her go. He was sure he would at some point.

Matt and Michael rolled into a chair and knocked it over. They didn't break the chair, but they did jostle some drinks. This caused one of the men at the table to get to his feet. Joe didn't recognize the man, so he must have come in on the stagecoach. The man got two good kicks in, one each to Matt and Michael. Neither kick were likely to do more damage than what the fighters were doing to each other. It meant they rolled away from the table. With no further issue to the table, the man sat back down.

Matt and Michael went back and forth without any good hits for several minutes. The crowd was starting to go back to their drinks and conversations. Jake looked at Joe again, but again received no signal to stop the fight. Joe let the fight go on a few minutes more. Aside from those at the closest tables, everyone else lost interest in the fight.

Joe stood up and went over to the two grown men rolling around on the floor. He grabbed both by the collar and pulled them apart.

"Let's go," Joe said as he dragged them towards the door.

"But-" Matt started.

"Nope," Joe said, "Not tonight."

Joe escorted them out of the saloon and off the sidewalk.

"You can come back and fix the chair you broke tomorrow when you are sober," Joe said before turning around and going back inside.

He sat back down in his place and took another sip of whiskey. Neither Matt nor Michael tried to come back inside. Everyone else was minding their own business. Joe could feel Dewhite's long stare but gave no indication of such. Dewhite went back to focusing on the game. It appeared it would be a long one. Jake offered Joe a refill in his whiskey and Joe nodded. There were still plenty of hours left in the night and Joe knew he would need to be here for the rest of that time.

# Chapter Two
## The Missing Wife

Sheriff Broddy was sitting at one of the tables in the saloon when Joe came downstairs the next afternoon. Broddy was eating. Joe sat down in the chair next to him.

"What brings you into my establishment today?" Joe asked.

"My deputy has been sitting out at the Grady property," Broddy answered, "And he says Mrs. Grady ain't been seen."

"Well, Len wasn't expected until today," Joe said.

"But everyone we talked to yesterday said she went home to be ready when he got there," Sheriff Broddy said, "She wasn't there when we were and she wasn't with anyone else either."

"I suppose it is something that should be looked into," Joe said, "Why me?"

"My deputy has other things to do," Sheriff Broddy answered, "And you don't have anything to do until late in the day."

"Fine," Joe said.

He might have said more but Miss. Edwards came in with a plate of food for him. She set it down in front of him before moving off to do something else.

"Good cooking," Broddy pointed his fork at his own plate.

"Yup," Joe said before he started eating.

They didn't speak for several minutes as they ate. The sheriff was done first, having started first.

"You got a new lady upstairs?" Broddy asked.

"Nope," Joe answered, "She said Lanaway suggested a

room here because he was full up."

"He was that," Broddy said, "But the stagecoach left this morning and she wasn't on it."

"She said she would be continuing west," Joe shrugged, "But she hasn't asked to use the room for anything other than sleeping."

"You gonna warn people away?" Broddy asked.

"I think she can do that on her own," Joe answered, "I only step into such matters if they try to make a scene about her saying no."

"Good," Broddy said, "You ain't much for sticking your neck out for anybody and I was hoping you weren't going to start now."

"My neck has been too exposed than I would like over my life," Joe said, "I prefer to turtle it these days."

"You been that way since I met you," Broddy said, "But sometimes a lady can make a man do strange things. I would prefer to know if there is that kind of trouble coming."

"I don't know why she didn't get on the stage," Joe said, "But if you want her to go, you can put her on the next one."

"She ain't caused trouble yet," Broddy said.

Joe nodded. They didn't say anything else as Joe finished eating. Broddy just stuck his hands in his pockets and leaned the chair back as he waited.

"Where else is there to look for Mrs. Grady?" Joe asked, "We tried Laine's Place and the Jarretts' yesterday."

"I thought we would start at the Grady place again," Broddy answered, "And go from there."

"Are we sure Mrs. Grady was ever at the house yesterday?" Joe asked, "Because everyone said that was where she was headed, but do we know if anyone saw her there?"

"No," Broddy said, "But hopefully we can figure that out."

Joe nodded.

When Joe was finished, he went back upstairs to his rooms. He put on his jacket and checked to make sure it looked good.

Then he made sure his hair was just right before carefully putting on his hat. Only when the mirror showed that he was ready did Joe leave his rooms. He went back downstairs.

Jake was now working with Miss. Edwards to get the saloon ready. He barely glanced up at Joe.

"Once again, open if I don't get back here in time," Joe said.

"Yes, sir," Jake replied.

Joe followed Sheriff Broddy out of the saloon. The sheriff's horse was waiting at the hitching post out front. Today there was no second horse.

"My deputy can't loan out his horse this time," Broddy said, "So, you need to get your own."

"That is fine," Joe said. He headed for the stable. William, the stable master, already had Joe's stallion ready for him.

"Broddy warned me you would need Journey," William said as he offered Joe the reins.

"Thank you," Joe said taking the reins. He led Journey out of the stables before mounting. Joe rode back to where Broddy was waiting on his horse outside the saloon. They got ready to head out of town when Doc McKaig came down the street in his wagon. He stopped next to them.

"Hello, Sheriff, McGraw. Have you talked to Mrs. Grady about what I am supposed to do with Len?" Doc McKaig asked.

"Not yet," Broddy answered.

"Well, you better do it soon," Doc McKaig said, "He isn't getting sweeter with time."

"We will bring it up when I find her," the sheriff said.

"She isn't out at Laine's place?" Doc McKaig asked, "That is where she usually goes when Len isn't in town."

"We asked Miss. Modahl when we stopped there on our way into town yesterday," Broddy said, "She said Mrs. Grady had left already. Everyone keeps saying she is likely to be a Laine's Place or at home. We haven't found her yet."

"Hopefully you find her soon," Doc McKaig said, "The sooner we get Len into the ground the better."

"If we don't find Mrs. Grady today, just bury him," the sheriff said, "We'll explain to her that we couldn't wait any longer. I am sure she will understand and the marker can be changed to whatever she wants later."

"Okay," Doc McKaig nodded, "Good luck with your search."

"We'll see you later," Broddy said.

Doc McKaig moved along. Broddy and Joe started moving in the direction of the Grady place.

The Grady place looked the same as when they left it the day before. There were no extra boot or hoof prints. The wind likely spread the dirt over what had been there the day before as they were not as clear as they had been. Broddy and Joe stopped at the hitching post and left their horses there.

The sheriff went to the porch but didn't step onto it. He stared at the dried blood on the boards and the dirt below. The sight of the blood seemed to mesmerize him.

"Blood speaking to you?" Joe asked stopping beside him.

"No," Broddy answered, "I have never been comfortable with the sight of blood."

"We can go in through the back," Joe said.

Broddy glanced at Joe before his attention was brought back to the blood.

"Most would mock me for admitting such a thing," Broddy said as he started moving toward the back of the house.

"We all have things we don't like or want to deal with," Joe said, "As much as trouble with blood is strange for a sheriff, there are much worse things to have troubles with."

"Well, I definitely couldn't have the same worries about clothing you do," Broddy said.

"When you pay as much as I do for clothing, you would take care of them too," Joe said.

"Not on my salary," Broddy said.

They reached the back at the house, but instead of heading for the door Broddy went toward the stables. The door was open. Joe followed Broddy inside. Their eyes took a moment to adjust. There were two stall doors open of the four stalls. Joe could not hear any animals. They walked through the stable without seeing anything out of the ordinary, except for the emptiness.

"I believe the Gradys had two horses," Sheriff Broddy said, "And Len would have taken one for his trip."

"She would have taken the second one when she went to Laine's Place," Joe said.

"But to leave the doors open?" Sheriff Broddy asked.

"That does seem strange," Joe answered. He looked into the stall on the side he was on. Everything looked normal as if the only thing wrong was the forgotten door. Joe turned to move out of the stall when something caught his attention and he turned back. Stepping farther into the stall, he bent over being careful of his clothing and picked up the item. It was a ripped piece of cloth. There was a pattern on it as if from a woman's dress.

"What is it?" the sheriff asked. Joe offered the piece to him. Broddy took it and examined it closely.

"Just shows she was in here," Joe said, "Which isn't strange since she lives here."

"But to have ripped like that involves a struggle," Sheriff Broddy said.

"If Len had taken his horse with him, wouldn't it have come back here for food and shelter?" Joe asked.

"One would think so," Sheriff Broddy answered, "But it doesn't seem to be here."

"Anything in the other side?" Joe asked.

"I didn't see anything," Sheriff Broddy answered, "But you can look."

He stepped out of the way so Joe could leave the stall and go into the other one. Joe checked over the stall, but nothing caught his eye.

"Nothing," Joe said as he stepped back out.

"To leave the doors open suggests leaving in a hurry," Sheriff Broddy said, "I would almost say that leaving both doors open would suggest that two people left in a hurry, but Len is dead. So, who would the other person be?"

"Len was found on the front porch," Joe said, "That suggests he didn't bring his horse around back. It might have been someone else who stabled their horse here."

"But what happened to that person and Mrs. Grady?" Sheriff Broddy asked.

Joe shrugged because neither of them had the answer to that. They left the stable and went to the house. The sheriff opened the back door and Joe followed him into the kitchen. Everything was the same as the last time Joe had been there.

"Looks like she was expecting someone for tea," Sheriff Broddy said, "But never got as far as pouring it."

"Maybe Mrs. Grady saw the murder and is hiding at Laine's Place," Joe said.

"Miss. Modahl would have said something if Mrs. Grady was there," Sheriff Broddy said, "But we will check it out again in case something has changed there. Where did you find the stud?"

"Under the settee in the living room," Joe answered.

Sheriff Broddy headed into the hallway and he turned into the doorway of the living room. Joe followed Broddy but stopped in the doorway. Broddy was wandering the room and even got down to look under the settee. He didn't find anything, even checking in between the cushions of the settee. Broddy seemed close to giving up when he went over to the window and stood there looking out.

"Something must have happened that let Mrs. Grady know Len was out there," Sheriff Broddy said, "If she is worried about the murderer coming after her, it will be much harder to find her."

Joe didn't respond as the sheriff seemed to be talking more to himself than to Joe and he didn't want to interrupt any thought processes. Broddy did not say anything more as he stared out the window. Joe waited.

"Why wouldn't she have opened the door for Len?" Sheriff Broddy asked after several minutes had passed, "She could definitely have seen him from a distance and known he was coming. Unless she was distracted."

"If there was someone else here, she was likely distracted," Joe said.

"Yes," Sheriff Broddy said. As much as Broddy answered Joe, he didn't seem to notice Joe.

It was several more minutes of Broddy being distracted before he suddenly looked around as if he was now aware of his surroundings. With a slight shake of his head, Broddy started towards the doorway. Joe moved out of the way. They went back to the kitchen and out the door.

Joe followed Broddy around the house to where their horses were waiting. They mounted and started back down the road. Broddy rode without talking and Joe did not bother to try to make conversation. They rode until Laine's Place came in sight. They once again left their horses at the hitching post and headed toward the door.

Miss. Modahl was the one who opened the door and stepped outside.

"Good afternoon, Sheriff," Miss. Modahl said, "Did you find Mrs. Grady?"

"No," Sheriff Broddy answered, "We are currently searching for her. Have you heard from her?"

"No," Miss. Modahl shook her head, "Not since she left."

"When she left here was she wearing anything with this material?" Sheriff Broddy asked showing Miss. Modahl the piece of fabric from the stable. Miss. Modahl looked at it.

"That looks like it is from the skirt she was wearing," Miss. Modahl said, "Is she in danger?"

29

"We don't know," Sheriff Broddy answered, "That is one of the reasons we want to find her as well as Doc McKaig is looking for answers to as to how Len wanted to be laid to rest."

"Unfortunately, she left yesterday morning and we have not heard from her since then," Miss. Modahl said, "If she does show up, we will redirect her to you."

"Thank you," Sheriff Broddy said, "One more question. Was Mrs. Grady expecting someone for tea yesterday?"

"She didn't say anything about expecting anyone," Miss, Modahl answered, "Only that she was preparing the house for Mr. Grady's return. She didn't mention anyone else visiting her."

"Do you know anyone she would go stay with if she was going to hide?" Joe asked.

"No, Mr. McGraw," Miss. Modahl answered, "Usually if she was not at home, she would stay here. Mrs. Grady did not stay with her friends in town."

"And there was nowhere else and no one else she would have stayed with?" Joe asked.

"No," Miss. Modahl shook her head.

"Thank you for answering our questions," Broddy said.

"You are welcome," Miss. Modahl said.

Broddy and Joe went back to their horses. They mounted and rode away.

"Mrs. Grady isn't at Laine's Place," Broddy said, "If she was, Amy would have given some sign of it."

"So, where now?" Joe asked.

"Back into town," Sheriff Broddy answered.

Joe took Journey back to the stables. William was busy with other horses, so Joe took care of his horse. Broddy had gone off to his office to check in with his deputy. Once he was finished in the stable, Joe went to the saloon. There he found Jake and Miss. Edwards working to get things ready for the night.

In his look around, Joe almost missed McPherson and Henczel sitting at a table near the back of the room. They were talking low enough Joe still would have missed them. Jake and Miss. Edwards were ignoring the men as they did their work. Since they made no signal for Joe to join them as they usually did when they met in the saloon, he headed upstairs. In his rooms, Joe took off his hat and coat before making sure his clothes and hair had not been messed up while he followed the sheriff around.

When he felt he was presentable, Joe went back downstairs. This time McPherson caught Joe's attention and signalled for him to come over. Joe kept the sigh from coming out as he went over to the table. He sat down at the table.

"We came to talk to you and Jake said you were off with the sheriff," McPherson said, "Again."

"He once again was looking to have a council member along," Joe answered.

"Still not willing to tell me why?" McPherson asked.

"Weren't you supposed to ask the sheriff about the what?" Joe asked.

"He wasn't willing to tell me," McPherson answered.

"Then why should I tell you about it?" Joe asked.

"The public's right to know," McPherson answered.

"What about the privacy of the people involved?" Joe asked.

"I am a newspaper man," McPherson answered, "I believe strongly in the public's right to know."

"Sounds like one of those ladies who have nothing better to do than gossip," Joe said.

"Except that he publishes it rather than spreading word of mouth," Henczel said, "It is hard to use name calling to stop a newspaper man from looking into a story."

"Well, appealing to his sense of decency hasn't worked so far," Joe said.

"Since the only story I have for publishing in the newspaper tomorrow is Mrs. Gilbert's latest publishing endeavor, I am looking for something else to add," McPherson said.

"Put Ed, here, up for mayor," Joe said.

"No, thank you," Henczel said, "I am happy to let Mr. Cheshire continue to be mayor."

"You'll just let him continue to be mayor?" Joe asked.

"If I actually put my name in for mayor, I am very likely to take the position from him," Henczel answered, "And I don't want to do that as he has little else in his life. Since he had to leave his farm and come out here, he hasn't had work in the same manner."

"He wouldn't have left his farm if he could have still worked it," McPherson said.

"I read the story you wrote about his history when he ran for mayor the first time," Joe said, "And about how his leg was damaged. Using a shotgun on someone does that."

"He never told me about it being a shotgun," McPherson said, "When did he say that was the cause? He never specified how he became a cripple. Who shot him?"

"He said it while he was here having a drink for celebrating his appointment to mayor," Joe answered.

"This is the first time you have told a story," McPherson said, "Did he tell you who used the shotgun on him."

"Yes," Joe answered, "He hadn't stopped at one drink that night and so he told me several stories about his life that you missed in your article."

"Well, you are in a position to set the record straight," McPherson said.

"But if he didn't tell you the stories to begin with, there must have been a reason," Joe said, "And it really isn't my job to tell other people's stories."

"I'll bet you know more than your share," Henczel said, "Because with booze in them, people say more than they should."

"Doesn't mean I have to repeat them," Joe said.

"Of course not," Henczel said, "I wasn't saying you should. Kevin, here, was saying you should tell him some."

"Doesn't change my stance on the matter," Joe said.

"Maybe you need to get this guy drunk," Henczel said to McPherson.

"I've watched him drink," McPherson said, "I don't know what it would take to get him drunk, but I am pretty sure there isn't enough booze in this place to do it."

"No one is that good at holding their liquor," Henczel said, "Usually after five or six bottles, you find out there is a limit to what they can handle."

"The newspaper doesn't make enough for me to buy five or six bottles to feed someone in hopes of getting stories out of them," McPherson said, "Otherwise I might try it."

"Now I know better than to get drunk when you are around," Joe said.

"I doubt you would say anything anyway," McPherson said, "You have worked hard to train yourself not to tell stories, whether they are yours or someone else's."

"With good reason," Joe said, "So, what is Mrs. Gilbert getting published?"

"I would tell you but it is much more to my satisfaction for you to buy a newspaper to find out," McPherson said.

"Fair enough," Joe said.

The door swung open and Scarlett stepped inside. She didn't look around. Instead she went straight up the stairs. Joe watched her without completely realizing he did it until he turned back and saw that McPherson and Henczel had done the same.

"New girl?" Henczel asked.

"Paying guest," Joe answered, "Because Lanaway said he was full when she tried to check in."

"The stagecoach left this morning, so he should have room now," Henczel said.

"I'm not sure why she wasn't on it," Joe replied.

"Was she supposed to be?" Henczel asked.

"She said she was traveling west," Joe answered, "To me that would suggest continuing the journey on the next stagecoach."

"She hasn't caused any trouble yet?" Henczel said.

"I don't know of any trouble involving her," Joe said.

"I'm surprised," Henczel said, "I would have thought you would be her first target."

"Oh, she started that last night," Joe said, "She might have done more but she didn't like to watch Michael and Matt go at each other."

"Really?" Henczel asked, "She doesn't seem like the sort put off by such behaviour."

"I doubt she is," Joe answered, "But she wants people to believe she is."

"So, you aren't falling for it all?" Henczel asked.

"Would you?" Joe asked.

"Definitely would be," Henczel answered.

"Then you understand the situation," Joe said.

"Is there a story here?" McPherson asked.

"Not yet," Henczel answered, "But it may come to that."

"I hope not," Joe said.

"Hasn't stopped it from coming to that," Henczel said.

"I know," Joe said with a long sigh.

Sheriff Broddy entered the saloon.

"Maybe he needs help from a council member again," McPherson said.

The sheriff came over to the table.

"You look like trouble," Broddy said looking around at the three men.

"Not yet," Henczel said, "But we could be if you need us to be."

"I have enough troubles without you making more," Broddy said.

"Tell us about them," McPherson said.

"Normally I wouldn't tell you anything," Broddy said, "But this time it might help to tell you about it."

"Okay," McPherson said.

"Mrs. Grady is missing," the sheriff said.

"What did Len have to say about the matter?" McPherson asked.

"Unfortunately, he isn't willing to tell us anything," Broddy answered.

"Then how do you know she is missing?" McPherson asked.

"Because no one has seen her since yesterday morning and she isn't anywhere she would usually be found," Broddy answered, "Unless you know something about where she could be that I don't."

"And you think I would keep such a thing a secret?" McPherson asked.

"No," Broddy answered, "But I ask anyway just in case."

"If she isn't at home, she stayed at Laine's Place," McPherson said, "Or at least as far as I know. With Len arriving home yesterday afternoon with everyone else, she would have been home to meet him. Len is never one to clam up or not answer questions."

"Usually he would be willing to talk, but not this time," Broddy said.

"Have you thought that he might have something to do with her disappearance?" McPherson asked.

"I know he has nothing to do with it," Broddy answered, "But if you spread the word I am looking for Mrs. Grady, others may be willing to tell me if they have seen her."

"I can do that," McPherson said, "When was she last seen?"

"Yesterday morning at Laine's Place," Broddy answered.

"And she didn`t make it home?" McPherson asked.

"There are signs that she did make it home," Broddy answered, "But she isn't there now and she hasn't been there since sometime yesterday."

"Okay," McPherson said, "I will see what people have to say. Did you question the Jarretts?"

"I have spoken with them twice," Broddy answered, "They don't know what could have happened to her."

"Did she stop in at the general store?" McPherson asked.

"Mrs. Gilbert says she hasn't seen Mrs. Grady," Broddy answered.

"If you have already asked everyone, why did need me to spread around that you are searching for her?" McPherson asked.

"I haven't asked everyone, just the obvious ones," Broddy answered, "Most of us end up at the general store or visit friends regularly, so it would make sense to talk to those people when looking for someone."

"I guess this story is good for tomorrow's paper," McPherson said as he got to his feet, "It can fit in beside the announcement about Mrs. Gilbert's publishing endeavor."

"Good," Broddy said.

"Then I have some work to do," McPherson said, "Talk to y'all later."

McPherson headed out of the saloon.

"Anything else you need?" Joe asked.

"No, I was just looking for McPherson," Broddy answered, "And now that I have talked to him, I thought I could use a drink."

"What do you want?" Joe asked as he got to his feet.

"Beer is fine," Broddy answered as he sat down in the chair McPherson has just vacated.

"I'll take one as well if you are pouring," Henczel said.

Joe went to the bar. He poured two beers and a scotch then brought the drinks back to the table. He sat down with them.

"So, Len is dead?" Henczel asked.

"Why do you say that?" Broddy asked.

"Because that would be the only reason you would be

looking for Mrs. Grady and Len wouldn't be willing to tell you anything," Henczel answered, "If he were alive, he would be willing to tell you anything you want to know. He has never been one to clam up."

"He was found with his own knife in him on his front porch," Broddy said, "I was hoping to talk to Mrs. Grady before I announced to the rest of the world."

"I'll keep my mouth shut," Henczel said, "But all McPherson needs to do is ask Doc McKaig and you aren't going to have a choice about word getting out."

"I know," Broddy said.

"There has been nothing to suggest to McPherson that he should talk to Doc McKaig," Joe said, "Otherwise he would have already gone there. And nothing you just said to him would direct him there."

"As long as he doesn't cross paths with Doc McKaig," Henczel said.

Broddy nodded before taking another drink of beer. The three of them were quiet as they drank. Joe only took a sip from his drink while the other two took mouthfuls.

Jake was still working to set things up, but Miss. Edwards had finished her cleaning and went off to start supper. Joe also noticed that the pieces of broken chair were gone. He figured Matt must have come and gotten them so he could fix the chair. That was the usual deal.

"DeWhite going to be holding his several-day game starting today?" Broddy asked.

"You would have to ask him," Joe answered, "I only provide the table and the booze."

"I was wondering because there is no one new in town to join the game," Broddy said.

"I would say might be a bigger problem if the ranchers didn't have money currently in their pockets," Joe said, "Even those who know they need money for later are likely to spend some they shouldn't on useless stuff."

"So, you think the game will go ahead?" Broddy asked.

"Yes," Joe answered, "But for specifics you have find and ask Jason."

"He'll be around in a while if the game is happening," Broddy said, "So, it shouldn't hard to find him."

"Up to you," Joe said.

"Been a while since I watched a game," Henczel said, "Maybe I'll stick around."

Joe shrugged.

Miss. Edwards came out of the kitchen with a plate of food for Joe. She set it in front of him.

"Will anyone else be eating?" Miss. Edwards asked.

"I'll pay for a plate, Marlo," Broddy answered.

"You eat too many meals here and Amy will start to wonder if you have lost interest in her," Miss. Edwards said with a laugh.

"No, she knows her place in my life," Broddy said, "And I am not out there for most of my meals anyway."

"Then I will get you a plate," Miss. Edwards said.

"I'm fine with my drink," Henczel said.

"Okay," Miss. Edwards said before she headed back into the kitchen. Jake followed her so he could eat in the kitchen. Joe had started eating while they were talking. A moment later Miss. Edwards came out with a plate for Broddy, who gave her some money in exchange for it.

"Is your guest going to eat supper as well?" Henczel asked.

"She asked for her meal in her room," Miss. Edwards answered, "I was going to take hers up in a few minutes."

"She doesn't seem very sociable," Henczel said.

"Some people are like that," Miss. Edwards said. She went back into the kitchen.

Henczel looked at Joe, who just shrugged.

"I haven't seen her much," Joe said, "She was down for a while last night and she went through earlier."

"Do you need to see more of her?" Broddy asked.

"Just answering his question," Joe answered.

"My advice is to stay away from her," Broddy said.

"Of course, that is your advice," Henczel said, "But really who wouldn't fall out of line for her?"

"I wouldn't," Broddy said.

"Keep telling yourself that," Henczel said.

Miss. Edwards came out of the kitchen with another plate, but this time she headed up the stairs.

"What about the rest of the ladies upstairs?" Henczel asked.

"They either come down for supper or they find somewhere else to eat," Joe answered, "The only way Miss. Edwards would take their supper upstairs for them is if they paid her to."

"Easier to just come down for the meal," Henczel said.

"That is how they feel so far," Joe said, "The only time they pay is if they are not feeling well."

"That does make sense," Henczel said.

"I don't provide anything to the women," Joe said, "Anything they want, they pay for. I also don't direct anyone to them. They have to find it themselves."

"Leaves you not at fault for anything that happens," Henczel said.

"That is how Joe works his life," Broddy said, "Not sticking his neck out for anybody."

"You say that as if you approve," Henczel said.

"I do," Broddy said, "Because then I know where he stands in all situations, which makes my job easier."

"No wonder you are warning him away from his guest," Henczel said.

Miss. Edwards came down the stairs and went back into the kitchen. Joe finished his food and pushed his plate away. He took a sip of his drink. The conversation between Broddy and Henczel continued while Joe let his thoughts wander.

He was not sure how long had passed when he realized the conversation had stopped. As he came back to the present, he noticed it was not because they were waiting for him. Instead it was because DeWhite had come in and Broddy was getting up to talk to him.

"So, a game will happen," Henczel said, "Even if it doesn't last days."

"He usually holds a game here every night," Joe said.

Joe gathered up his dishes as well as Broddy's dishes and took them into the kitchen. Jake and Miss. Edwards were still eating along with a couple of the ladies from upstairs. He left the dishes near the dish pan. Then he went back out to the main room. Joe went behind the bar to serve drinks until Jake could come out.

Sheriff Broddy stepped out of the saloon and the door swung shut behind him. He felt his pockets for his tobacco pouch and rolling papers, but he could not find them. Instead Broddy stuck his hands in his pockets and stepped off the sidewalk and into the street. He headed down towards his office. Most of the other buildings were dark as the occupants were either headed to bed or off to wherever they were spending their evening.

The light in his office was on as his deputy was sitting beside the stove. Broddy could see him through the window because the shutter had been left open. It looked lonely from Broddy's point of view. But he already knew that and chose it. His mentor has told him what would happen if he became sheriff of this town rather than choosing to train for another profession. But the call of justice and helping people was too much for Broddy to become anything else. Just as he wanted to find justice for Len Grady.

Joe sat at on his stool at the end of the bar. DeWhite had the game going. Miss. Karina was sitting near him. Henczel had found himself a seat where he could watch the game. The saloon was busy as usual. Joe only helped Jake out the few times when too many people came to the bar for a drink at once. Miss. Edwards didn't come out to help as she was not needed.

As Joe took a sip of his drink, Scarlett sat down on the next stool. She didn't have a drink this time, nor did she appear to be ready to order one. Tonight she was wearing a purple dress with a lower collar.

"It seems quieter tonight," Scarlett said.

"Most people spent their money last night," Joe said, "And won't be back until after pay day."

"Not even to watch the game," Scarlett said nodded towards the poker game.

"It doesn't matter if they come to watch tonight or tomorrow as the game is set to go for a couple days," Joe said.

"You don't seem interested in watching them play," Scarlett said.

"I have seen plenty of games," Joe said, "And I have seen all of the current players play."

"So, if poker doesn't interest you, what does?" Scarlett asked as she leaned closer to Joe.

"Plenty of things," Joe said. He used his glass to have something between him and her. She smiled at his attempt at space.

"Like what?" Scarlett asked.

"You have no interest in poker?" Joe asked.

"I never really saw the point," Scarlett answered, "No one has ever explained it to me, so I really don't know how it is played."

"Mostly it is betting on what cards turn up," Joe said, "The skill comes into the game in making your opponents believe you have a different hand than you really have."

"Do you play?" Scarlett asked.

"I have once or twice," Joe answered, "But I was not good enough to want to play much more than that. I also chose not to lose money in the matter."

"You seem to be such a hard man to read, I would think you would be good at poker and be able to get plenty of money from it," Scarlett said.

"I have too many tells," Joe said.

"Like what?" Scarlett asked.

"I'll let you figure them out yourself," Joe answered, "That seems like your type of thing."

"You think so?" Scarlett asked.

"I think so," Joe answered.

Scarlett's smiled widened and more of her teeth showed. Joe felt the right side of his mouth turn upward in response. He once again put his glass between them and took a drink. Scarlett leaned a little farther forward so Joe could see further down her dress. His eyes were drawn there whether he wanted to or not, though he probably didn't fight it as much as he should have. When he did manage to move to looking into her eyes, Joe found laughter in them. He knew he was falling into her trap and he also knew there was nothing he could do to stop.

# Chapter Three
## The Bootprints

Joe closed the door behind him before moving down the hallway to his own rooms. Inside he changed into fresh clothes after washing up. Only once the mirror showed he was ready did Joe leave his rooms. He went down to the main room.

The poker game was still going, but the audience was down to only a couple people. DeWhite was still in his usual spot. Miss. Karina was still near him but in a different dress. Henczel was gone. Jake was still behind the bar. Joe went over to the bar.

"Anything to report?" Joe asked.

"No," Jake answered, "Marlo was in earlier and I think she is in the kitchen making lunch."

"I'll take over for you and you can get some sleep before tonight," Joe said.

"Okay," Jake said. He came out from behind the bar and Joe took his place. Jake did not leave the main room. Instead he sat down at a table.

No one was really interested in getting anything from the bar at that moment, so Joe did some cleaning, organizing, and taking inventory. He was only a few minutes in when Miss. Edwards came out with a couple of plates of food. She gave one to Jake and brought the other to Joe. She went back to the kitchen. Joe stood and ate his lunch.

When they were both finished, Jake took the dishes into the kitchen. He did not come back to the main room. Joe went back to his make work. When there was nothing else for him to do, Joe leaned against the bar and watched the game from that distance. He was not close enough to actually see how anyone was doing. DeWhite might have been winning as usual, but Joe couldn't tell.

The door swung open and Shorty stepped inside. He went to the table near the game and turned a chair so it was facing the game. Then he sat down in the chair. Shorty watched the game for a few minutes until he figured out who was winning and how things were going. Once he had it sorted out, Shorty seemed to lose interest in the game as if he was only there because he was expected to be. He lifted his boot to rest on his knee and started to run his thumb over the v pattern on the sole.

Joe found himself watching Shorty Jennings rub the bottom of his boot as that was the most activity going on that was visible. Shorty had long ago rubbed a v into the sole of his boot and the lines were clear across the room. Something tickled the back of Joe's brain, but he could not think of what it would be. If it had to do with the players, he would have felt it earlier, so it must have had something to do with Shorty in particular. Except that Joe had never had anything to do with Shorty.

One of the players got up and came over to the bar. Joe refilled his glass. The player returned to the game. All activity was over again. Joe went back to leaning on the bar. His eyes wandered over the room before once again resting on the only movement he could see, which was Shorty's thumb going back and forth along the v. It was hypnotizing and Joe found himself losing minutes.

Joe was brought out of it with the opening of the door. Sheriff Broddy stepped inside. He came over to the bar.

"I can't help in any searching today," Joe said, "I have to work."

"I figured," Broddy said, "Seen the newspaper for today?"

"No," Joe answered.

The sheriff placed it on the bar for Joe to see it. The top headline was indeed about Mrs. Grady being missing. The second headline was about Mrs. Gilbert's book of poetry. Joe skimmed the article on Mrs. Grady. Nowhere did it mention Len being dead.

"Has it helped?" Joe asked.

"I have had a few people come by this morning with the latest gossip about Mrs. Grady," Broddy answered, "But either I already know it or it is pure gossip without any truth behind it. I left my deputy to listen to any other stories people might bring in. Maybe someone else will have something useful, maybe not. In the meantime, I thought I would sit in here for a while."

"That is fine," Joe said, "Plenty of others will come through here today."

Broddy sat down on one of the stools.

"So, she writes poetry," Joe said as he skimmed the second article.

"You didn't know?" Broddy asked.

"I've never paid attention," Joe said with a shrug.

"With all your reading, you never noticed she writes poetry?" Broddy asked.

"I don't tend to read poetry," Joe answered, "Most of what I read is philosophy."

"I suppose that explains a few things," Broody said, "Though plenty of the poetry I have read borders on the philosophical."

"They both focus on various aspects of life," Joe said, "Like meaning and purpose."

"Do you read philosophy because you have figured those out or because you are still trying to figure it out?" Broddy asked.

"I read it because I find it interesting," Joe answered, "Not so much because I feel the need to figure life out. People who read poetry don't usually read it for the insights in life."

"I would never read philosophy for fun," Broddy said.

"To each his own," Joe said.

"Some say that those who don't like poetry just haven't met the right poem yet," Broddy said.

"That could be true," Joe said, "But I can't say it is for certain because I haven't found the right poem yet."

There was a shout from the poker game. Joe and Broddy looked over in time to see DeWhite and Emerson stand up and push their chairs back; neither man had a gun but they both had knives. Broddy got up from his stool and headed for the game.

"Cheater," Emerson's tone was full of contempt.

"It was in the rules when you sat down," DeWhite said, "They haven't changed."

"Cheater," Emerson hissed.

"Emerson," Broddy said.

"What!" Emerson turned to the sheriff.

DeWhite inched his knife out.

"Walk away," Broddy said.

Emerson hesitated while DeWhite held his hand still.

"Walk away," Broddy's tone was firm.

Emerson turned back to the game, but it was only long enough to take the rest of his money off the table before stalking out of the saloon.

DeWhite let his knife slide back into its place before he sat down. Everyone went back to the game. Broddy watched the game for a moment more before moving back to the bar. He sat down again.

"Maybe reading Mrs. Gilbert's volume of poetry you will find the poem," Broddy said.

"I may read it," Joe said, "But I am not sure about finding that specific poem. Not that I would block it if it was there."

"I found mine years ago when I came across a poem by Kalut," Broddy said, "It spoke to me while talking about footprints in dirt. Not sure what happened to the book

I found it in, but I haven't found it since. However, I remember it well."

"Footprints," Joe said. His eyes lost focus for a moment as his mind went from the present moment to some memory.

"What about footprints?" Broddy asked. Joe came back to the moment and looked at Sheriff Broddy.

"Something was bothering me earlier and I couldn't think of what it was," Joe said, "It was footprints."

"And what about footprints?" Broddy asked.

Joe leaned closer to Broddy and lowered his voice.

"Shorty has a v on the sole of his boot," Joe said, "He had his foot up earlier and I saw it."

"Why would Shorty be out at the Grady place?" Sheriff Broddy also lowered his voice. He looked toward the game. Shorty was still sitting in the same spot. In fact, his boot was still resting on his leg with v mark visible.

"Only one way to figure that out," Joe said.

"But you can't leave your post," Sheriff Broddy said.

"I can see if Marlo would take it for a few minutes," Joe said. He straightened up and headed for the kitchen. Joe found Miss. Edwards sitting at the table with a book open in front of her.

"Sheriff Broddy would like my help for a few minutes," Joe said.

"That is fine," Miss. Edwards said as she put a marker in her place in the book. She got to her feet and followed Joe into the main room. Miss. Edwards went behind the bar. Sheriff Broddy was already on his way to where Shorty was sitting. He leaned down to say something quietly in Shorty's ear. Shorty hesitated a moment before getting up. He followed Broddy out the back door of the saloon. No one else noticed them leave as Joe followed them out.

Sheriff Broddy stopped and turned around. Shorty stopped to avoid hitting Sheriff Broddy before glancing over his shoulder at Joe. He slid sideways as if to get away, but found it only meant his back was against the outside wall of the saloon. Sheriff Broddy and Joe took up positions on either side of him to make sure Shorty could not run. Shorty glanced back and forth between the men. He swallowed.

"What can I help you with?" Shorty asked.

"We need you to give us some information," Sheriff Broddy answered.

"Not sure I can help you," Shorty said.

"I wouldn't be asking you if I didn't think you had the answers to my questions," Sheriff Broddy said.

"What about him?" Shorty pointed a thumb towards Joe.

"I'm just here in case I am needed to help you answer the questions," Joe answered.

Shorty tried to look like it did not bother him, but there was fear in his eyes. He did not say anything. His eyes moved back to Sheriff Broddy.

"You were out at the Grady place yesterday," Sheriff Broddy said.

"No, I wasn't," Shorty said.

"Why were you there?" Sheriff Broddy asked.

"I wasn't there," Shorty answered.

"I know you were there," Sheriff Broddy said.

"How do you know I was out at the Grady place?" Shorty asked.

"Your boot prints gave you away," Sheriff Broddy answered, "Now, answer the question."

"I was supposed to be pick up a shirt that Mrs. Grady was supposed to embroider for me," Shorty said, "She said it was ready a few days ago, but that was the first I had time to go. Miss. Modahl said Mrs. Grady was at home, so I went there. But I don't know where she is now."

"Did you see Len there?" Sheriff Broddy asked.

"No," Shorty answered, "I didn't see him at all."

"But you saw Mrs. Grady," Sheriff Broddy said.

"Yes," Shorty said, "But I didn't talk to her or get the shirt."

"Why?" Sheriff Broddy asked.

"Because she already had a guest," Shorty answered, "She never even knew I was ever there."

"How do you know someone else was there if she never knew you were?" Sheriff Broddy asked.

"I saw them through the window," Shorty answered, "I was just about to knock when I heard something that made me look. Mrs. Grady was there but she wasn't alone."

"Who else was there?" Sheriff Broddy asked.

"I'm not sure I should tell you," Shorty answered.

"You are going to get in trouble if you don't," Sheriff Broddy said.

"I am likely to get in trouble if I do," Shorty said, "He might kill me."

"If neither this person nor Mrs. Grady knew you were there, how can they know it was you who said anything?" Sheriff Broddy asked.

"He might still manage it," Shorty said.

"I can arrest you for not telling me," Sheriff Broddy said, "And when we find the person, he will know it was you. So, you might as well tell us in this situation where you won't be given away."

"Fine," Shorty answered, "It was Slick."

"McQueen?" Sheriff Broddy asked.

"Yes," Shorty answered.

"You saw Slick McQueen with Mrs. Grady through the window of the Grady place?" Sheriff Broddy asked.

"Yes," Shorty said with a nod.

"What would Slick McQueen be doing at the Grady's place?" Sheriff Broddy asked.

"Why would any man be at another man's house when he isn't home?" Shorty asked, "Mrs. Grady wasn't arguing."

Broddy glanced at Joe, who shrugged.

"That is what I saw," Shorty said, "That is the last I saw of Mrs. Grady. Len wasn't there."

"Fine," Sheriff Broddy said.

"Can I go now?" Shorty asked, "I don't know anything else."

"Fine," Sheriff Broddy answered.

Joe stepped back so Shorty could go passed him and back into the saloon. Broddy stood there a moment without saying anything. Joe did not interrupt his thought process.

"Slick would kill Len if Len had shown up during a time when Slick shouldn't have been there," Broddy said, "It also would explain why Mrs. Grady is missing."

"You'll have to go get Slick," Joe said, "Because he isn't likely to just show up if you ask, especially if he was the one who stabbed Len."

"Slick's camp is a distance from here," Broddy said, "Which is why I haven't bothered to try to arrest him for several of his crimes. To start now would mean arriving after dark and I would prefer to confront him during daylight. That leaves questioning him until tomorrow."

"Tomorrow I should be able to accompany you if you need," Joe said.

"I would appreciate the company," Broddy said, "You still have your gun, right? Because I haven't seen it in a while."

"I have it somewhere," Joe answered, "I was never good with it and I was only wearing it as a deterrent until I figured it was better not to, as some see a gun and feel the need to challenge the person. I prefer not to be challenged so I put the gun away."

"Well, bring it out for tomorrow because I don't want to be the only one armed while we walk into an outlaw's camp," Broddy said.

"I understand," Joe said, "I will find it before we head out tomorrow."

"Good," Broddy said. He headed inside and Joe followed him. Broddy sat back down on the stool at the bar. Joe took up his position behind the bar and let Miss. Edwards return to the kitchen.

"How about a beer?" Broddy asked.

Joe poured the beer and set it down in front of Broddy, who gave him the money for the drink. The game was going the same as when they had gone outside. Shorty was back to his seat, but this time both feet were on the floor.

"McPherson said he didn't know the mayor's limp was from a shotgun wound," Joe said.

"I'm surprised," Broddy said, "That would be the type of story McPherson likes to wheedle out of people. I know the story."

"I said something about it yesterday because I thought he would have heard the story," Joe said, "I was told it by the mayor during his drinking after he won the position, among other stories."

"You didn't share the rest of those stories, did you?" Broddy asked.

"Once he told me he hadn't heard the story, I didn't say anything more," Joe answered, "Those aren't my stories to share."

"Are there any stories that you share?" Broddy asked.

"Not if I can help it," Joe answered.

"I didn't think so," Broddy said.

The door opened and Henczel stepped inside. He looked around before coming over to where Broddy and Joe were.

"Beer?" Henczel asked as he sat down.

Joe poured a beer and set it in front of Henczel, who gave Joe the money for it.

"I had wondered where you had gone," Henczel said after he had a sip.

"Too many people showing up with too useless information," Broddy answered.

"What did you expect from letting McPherson put it out there?" Henczel asked.

"Help," Broddy answered.

Henczel shook his head.

"I know how well going to the public works," Broddy said, "But sometimes it works."

"How do you know if no one is bringing you important information if you aren't there to listen?" Henczel asked.

"I will hear what they have told my deputy later," Broddy answered.

"Doesn't give you much time to act on that information today," Henczel said.

"I'm not worried about that right now," Broddy said.

"Then you must not think she is in danger," Henczel said.

"All I know is that she isn't at home or any of the usual places she would be," Broddy said.

"But her husband is dead," Henczel said, "Shouldn't that make you worried for her safety?"

"It could be an issue," Broddy said.

"You know more about her location than you are saying," Henczel said, "Otherwise you aren't doing your job."

"Am I required to tell you everything involving the investigation?" Broddy asked.

"No," Henczel answered, "As long as I know you aren't abandoning a townsperson who is in trouble."

"Are you sure you aren't trying for mayor?" Joe asked.

"I told you I am not rushing Mr. Cheshire out of office," Henczel answered.

"Worried someone could probably come after you some day?" Broddy asked, "Because you never struck me as the type to make a lot of enemies."

"Anything is possible," Henczel answered.

One of the players took a break long enough to come over to the bar for a refill. Joe poured the drink. Then the player went back to the game. The next round started.

"Who is winning?" Henczel asked.

"DewWhite," Joe answered, "The only time he loses is when someone comes through town who is better than he is. Winning is why he plays."

One of the players pushed his chair back and got to his feet. He nodded to the other players before leaving the table. He came over to the bar and ordered a drink. Joe poured the drink and the man paid for it. The man tossed it down his throat in one go. After placing the glass back on the bar, the man left the saloon.

"One down," Henczel said.

"Second one down," Joe said, "The first went last night and was replaced shortly after he left."

"Anyone going to replace this one?" Henczel asked.

"At this point of the game, it isn't likely unless they are invited," Joe answered, "Or they show off the large amount of money they have with them."

"When does the next stagecoach come through?" Henczel asked.

"A couple days," Broddy answered, "The game will be over before then."

"But if there is someone to play against, DeWhite will start another game," Joe said.

"Do you get anything for letting them take over your business for days?" Henczel asked.

"They keep buying booze," Joe answered.

"No percentage of the winnings?" Henczel asked.

"No," Joe answered.

"Why?" Henczel asked, "Wouldn't it make sense for you to get something for taking up space in your business?"

"He has a game going on every night," Joe said, "And occasionally a multiple day game. Doesn't mean he rents the space."

The sound of drunk singing came from out in the street. It was a male voice as loud as he could and off tune.

"The woman of the east. She awaits the letter. Of her love who is far away. The man who headed west. To find his fortune for his love. His fortune in gold.

The woman of the east awaited word of her love. She

refused all offers of courting. As she knew her love would
return for her. The woman of the east had beauty of legend.
Many tried for her hand but her heart was traveling west
without her.

The woman of the east. She await the letter. Of her love
who is far away. The man who headed west. To find his
fortune for his love. His fortune in gold.

The man travelled west. The journey was hard. As his
greenness was turned to coldness. He rode hard as he
searched out his fortune. His heart remained with his love.

The fortune was not easily found as the man wanted.

The woman of the east. She await the letter. Of her love
who is far away, The man who headed west. To find his
fortune for his love. His fortune in gold."

Any other verses were cut off by the sound of a gunshot.
The sheriff was up and headed for the door in seconds.
Henczel followed immediately after him. The game stopped
as everyone looked toward the door. Joe went around the bar
and went outside after Sheriff Broddy and Henczel.

By the time Joe stepped out, Sheriff Broddy and Henczel
were standing in the street. Joe didn't immediately recognize
the man lying face down in the dirt. The shooter was not
visible. Other people were starting to come out of their
businesses to see what was going on. Sheriff Broddy bent
down to check on the man. Joe didn't see any blood, but it
could all be underneath the man.

Joe moved to the edge of the sidewalk and looked both
directions. There was no sign of any shooter. Or anyone
appearing to run away. Everyone was moving forward to see
what had happened. Joe could hear others coming out of the
saloon behind him. They did not move as close to the edge
of the sidewalk as he had but stayed behind him.

The man on the ground sat up slowly. He didn't seem to
be hurt as he dusted himself off. Joe noticed that he did not
have a gun nor was there one near him.

"Are you okay, Mr. Miller?" Mr. Lanaway asked from his position on the sidewalk outside the hotel.

"The bullet missed me," the man answered as he got the rest of the way to his feet, "I really didn't expect being shot at when I came out here."

"May I ask why you stepped outside?" the sheriff asked.

"To have a smoke," Mr. Miller answered, "I didn't want to smoke in the room with my son because it bothers him. There was someone singing but I couldn't see who it was. Then someone shot at me and I dived to avoid being hit."

"Unfortunately, you crossed paths with our phantom songster," Broddy said, "He tends to shoot at anyone who might see him and reveal his identity."

"I wasn't interested in him," Mr. Miller said, "I only wanted a smoke."

"Apparently, he didn't understand that," Broddy said, "We are sorry for this happening and hope the rest of your stay in our town is uneventful."

"I hope so too," Mr. Millar said, "I would like to have my smoke without worrying about my life."

The people who had come out behind Joe were starting to wander back inside. He could hear them. But he did not move.

The sheriff made sure Mr. Millar made it to the chair on the sidewalk outside the Lanaway Hotel. The people who had come out to see what happened started going back inside as there did not seem to be any more excitement for the moment. Henczel came over to Joe and then they went inside the saloon.

The game had restarted as all the players had returned to the table. Joe went back to being behind the bar and Henczel sat down on the stool he had been on before. Henczel finished the last of his beer.

"Perhaps another one," Henczel said as he put the glass back down.

Joe took the glass and poured more beer. When he finished, he moved it back to Henczel.

"I thought for sure we were going to find out who the phantom singer is," Henczel said, "Disappointing."

"Maybe someday we will," Joe said.

"Probably take someone taking a shot at him," Henczel said.

"Probably," Joe said.

Henczel took another drink rather than respond.

Scarlett came down the stairs and came towards the bar. Henczel saw her and vacated his stool to move to a table closer to the poker game. Scarlett smoothed the back of her dress before sitting down on a stool.

"Good afternoon," Scarlett said with a smile.

"Good afternoon," Joe replied. His lips curled upward slightly as if he had no control over them.

"What was with the shooting?" Scarlett asked.

"Just a local taking a pot-shot at a visitor," Joe answered, "Nothing to worry about."

"Is everyone okay?" Scarlett asked.

"No one was hurt," Joe answered.

"That is good," Scarlett said.

"It is," Joe said. He let the conversation fall as she seemed to be waiting for him to say more. The lull continued as Joe said nothing. His mind was blank as all thoughts about things had disappeared. He knew she wanted him to say things about how great last night was and how much it meant to him, but he had nothing to say on the matter.

The saloon doors opened and Broddy stepped inside. After a quick glance around, Broddy came over to the bar. He took his drink and then moved to sit at the table where Henczel was.

"It is busier in here today than usual," Scarlett said.

"People stayed to watch the game," Joe replied.

"Has anything interesting happened in the game?" Scarlett asked.

"Two people have left," Joe answered, "I don't know about in the game itself."

"Haven't you been paying attention?" Scarlett asked.

"Not really," Joe answered, "I am not really into watching poker games. It just doesn't interest me."

"Right, you are not into watching poker," Scarlett said.

"Right," Joe replied.

Someone from the poker game got up and came over to the bar. Joe refilled the drink. The man took his drink and went back to the game. By the time he was settled into his chair the next hand started.

Scarlett had watched the man go back to the game but then turned back to Joe. It seemed for a few moments that she would say something, but then once again she appeared to be waiting for him to continue the conversation. Joe said nothing. Scarlett put her hand on the bar as if she was going to tap her fingernails then she appeared to think better of it and just left her hand flat.

The noise from the game filled to void but even then it was not words, just sounds. The voices becoming the same as the rattling of chips or the shuffling of cards. Nothing came from the kitchen or from outside. Broddy and Henczel were merely drinking and not talking.

Scarlett shifted slightly on her stool. She worked to keep the frustration off her face, even as it kept creeping up. Lifting her hand off the bar, Scarlett put it in her lap and then clasped her hands together. She kept her eyes on Joe as she waited. Joe busied himself with taking an inventory. Scarlett put her hand back on the bar, but again managed to avoid drumming her fingers with impatience. Several times Scarlett held in a breath that might have turned into a sigh otherwise.

Another man pushed his chair back and stood up. But he didn't head over to the bar. Instead, he put his hat on and nodded to the rest of the players. He left the saloon. The last three players got ready for the next hand.

"Another player gone," Scarlett said, "I wonder how long the game is going to last now."

Joe gave a non-committal shrug and went back to what he was doing. Scarlett tapped her index finger once before she realized what she was doing and stopped. She crossed her arms over her chest instead. Joe did not appear to notice, even though he was very aware of every movement she made. It was better for both of them if he did not acknowledge there being anything between them. If he did anything to suggest otherwise, she would stay to make plans to stay and then there would be trouble.

Broddy got up and brought his glass over to the bar. He set it down. Joe refilled it. Broddy picked it up and he went back to the table with Henczel. Joe went back to what he was doing.

"I think I will have a drink as well," Scarlett said as she uncrossed her arms and rested her fingers on the edge of the bar.

"Whatever you are willing to pay for," Joe answered.

Scarlett fished into her pocket and then set the money on the bar. Joe took it and poured her a drink, which he set in front of her. Then he went back to the task he set for himself. Scarlett waited to see if he had any more to say before reaching for the glass. She took a sip of the drink and then set the glass down again.

Several minutes went by. Scarlett came close to setting her hand on the bar to tap her fingers but managed to stop herself. On the third attempt, Scarlett had brought her hand up, so she took another sip of her drink to make it look like she meant to raise her hand. When she set the glass down, she left her hand on it. This helped prevent her from tapping her fingers. Instead she found herself spinning the glass on the bar.

Scarlett took another sip to stop herself from moving the glass around. She set the glass back down on the bar and let her hand fall to her lap. Sitting there, she stared at Joe as if that would make him talk to her. However, Joe was busy being busy and pretending not to pay attention to her. Finally with a sigh, Scarlett took her drink and got up off the stool. She headed up the stairs.

Henczel and Broddy got up and moved over to the stools at the bar. As they settled, Joe finished his last bit of inventory.

"You know there are better ways to annoy a female?" Broddy asked.

"I know," Joe answered, "But it worked well enough."

"So, annoying her was your goal?" Henczel asked.

"More of the outcome of things," Joe answered, "I notice both of you kept your distance."

"We wouldn't want to interrupt a private conversation," Henczel said.

"Never stopped you before," Joe said.

The door of the saloon opened and McPherson stepped inside. He looked over the game before coming over to the bar.

"A drink?" Henczel asked.

"I'll certainly accept one," McPherson answered.

Henczel gave Joe the money. Joe poured the drink as McPherson sat down on the next stool.

"So, the phantom singer struck again," McPherson said.

"Actually, he missed," Broddy said.

"Who did he almost hit this time?" McPherson asked.

"Todd Millar," Broddy answered.

"Who?" McPherson asked.

"He is staying overnight and leaving tomorrow with his son," Broddy answered, "He happened to be stepping out for a smoke and the phantom singer thought he was out there to learn more about who was singing."

"He wasn't harm, though?" McPherson asked, "You said the phantom singer missed."

"He was not harmed," Broddy answered.

"Good," McPherson said.

"You weren't around during the phantom singer's performance," Henczel said, "It could be you."

"We were together when the last performance happened," McPherson said, "Unless I can throw my voice, it isn't possible."

"Can you throw your voice?" Broddy asked.

"No," McPherson answered, "I never learned how. It did seem like a fun thing to be able to do when I saw a man at the circus do it when I was a child."

"None of the rest of us thought the phantom singer being able to do such a thing, except you," Henczel said.

"Just because I thought about it doesn't mean I am the phantom singer," McPherson said, "For one, you have all seen me during times when the singing is happening and two, I can sing better than that."

"I'm pretty sure the phantom singer can sing better than he does," Broddy said, "But if he did sing it properly, we would recognize his voice and then know who he is, which he has worked hard not to have happen."

"It doesn't worry you that we still don't know who he is?" McPherson asked.

"Not really," Broddy answered, "I am only worried about whether he hits anyone. I would prefer he didn't shoot at people, but as long as he continues to miss them it isn't a bad as it could be."

"In other words, as long as everyone is safe, out of tune singing is okay," McPherson said.

"Correct," Broddy said.

"That is his job," Henczel said, "To protect the people of the town. Unfortunately, being forced to listen to bad singing isn't going to do us physical harm, as much as it will chip away at our sanity."

"And when we start shooting at the singer?" McPherson asked

"Have you purchased a gun since the last time I checked?" Broddy asked.

"No," McPherson answered,

"When you decide to get one, let me know so I can be more watchful during those times when there is singing," Broddy said.

"Are you sure no one else is likely to do it for me?" McPherson asked.

"I like to keep track of those in town who own guns and those who are likely to set them off," Broddy said, "So far, you are the only one suggesting shooting people, which I will continue to let you discuss as long as there is no chance of convincing someone who does own a gun."

Someone from the game stood up. They brought their glass over to the bar. Joe refilled it. They went back to the game with their drink and arrived in time for the next deal.

"They are down to three," McPherson said, "How long do you think that can last?"

"Until late tomorrow afternoon," Joe answered.

"Why are you that exact?" McPherson asked.

"Because that is usually how long the game goes on for," Joe answered, "I have seen enough of them to know when they end. I am pretty sure they stop because they can't stay awake any longer, rather than anyone running out of money."

"DeWhite doesn't just get it all?" Henczel asked.

"Sometimes," Joe answered, "But if he does, the game doesn't last as long as usual. The current players are more likely to play to a draw. The only thing that might change is if one has a run of bad luck."

"So, there isn't much expected for the next several hours?" Henczel asked.

"Not until late tonight or tomorrow," Joe answered.

"Then I should go find myself supper," Henczel said. He finished his drink before standing up.

"I have someplace to be as well," Broddy said as he got to his feet.

"Not going to eat what Miss. Edwards has cooked?" Joe asked.

"I have a better offer," Broddy answered with a smile before he and Henczel left the saloon.

"Don't have a place to go?" Joe asked.

"Not for another hour at least," McPherson answered, "But I'm not looking for a meal during that time. I'll have another drink though."

Joe refilled McPherson's glass.

"I thought Emerson would have lasted longer," McPherson said.

"He accused DeWhite of cheating and left the game," Joe answered.

"Again?" McPherson asked.

"Not sure why he decided to play after the last time," Joe said, "Unless someone talked him into it. DeWhite wouldn't bother since he prefers not to be accused in the middle of a game."

"I am sure that having gone through it twice, he will make sure it doesn't happen again," McPherson said.

Miss. Edwards came out of the kitchen with a plate of food. She brought it to Joe before going back to the kitchen. Joe came around the bar to sit on a stool while he ate.

"Has the sheriff made any progress in finding Mrs. Grady?" McPherson asked.

"He came in here to avoid people who were bringing him information about her," Joe answered, "But it didn't sound like there was anything new."

"I did try to help," McPherson said, "He should know that people can get overeager when asked for help."

"He did seem to expect it," Joe said, "He left his deputy to deal with it while he came here."

"I suppose that is one way to deal with the problem," McPherson said.

"Yup," Joe said.

# Chapter Four
# The Ride Out

The gun holster was uncomfortable on Joe's hip as he stepped out of the saloon. It made him want to limp but he repressed the impulse. The fact that the holster wrinkled the fabric of his pants pained him more. He also knew it would only get worse with the ride. He sighed as stepped down of the sidewalk. He headed for the stable, where William had Journey ready.

When Joe rode out of the stable, Sheriff Broddy was sitting on his horse outside. He had a rifle with him to go along with the holstered pistol on each hip. Joe might have felt underpowered, except his knowledge about his level of ability meant he would just look like an idiot if he had tried to arm himself in such a way.

"Ready?" Broddy asked.

"No," Joe answered, "But I'm not sure there is a ready when preparing oneself for walking into an outlaw's lair."

"Then let's go," Broddy said.

They started along the road with Broddy picking the direction and Joe followed along.

"Your deputy didn't demand to come along when you told him you were venturing into the hideout of an outlaw?" Joe asked.

"No," Broddy answered, "In fact, he seemed relieved when I told him he was to stay and watch the town."

"Not very adventurous of him," Joe said.

"If you mean cowardly," Broddy said, "I would have stayed here if I had the option. Wouldn't you?"

"Not really," Joe answered, "And I meant adventurous, not cowardly."

"It doesn't bother you to walk into an outlaw's hideout?" Broddy asked.

"Overall, no," Joe answered, "The worst that could happen is they would kill me."

"You have no fear of death?" Broddy asked.

"I have had plenty of time to enjoy life," Joe answered, "So, it doesn't matter to me."

"You still have plenty of life left," Broddy said.

"And plenty of live for," Joe said, "But I also have lived enough that I don't have any regrets if I die."

"I suppose I can understand that on some level," Broddy said, "But on every other one I don't get it."

"You're seeing things from the other end of things," Joe said.

"Our ages aren't that far apart," Broddy said.

"Probably why you understand it on one level," Joe said.

Broddy fell into a thoughtful pause in the conversation and Joe didn't interrupt. Instead Joe let his attention wandered to the landscape. The town had been left behind, however, they were still going through ranchlands. Aside from the road, the ground was planted in short grass, which the cows enjoyed. Some of the properties had fences and others didn't.

The ground was not flat but its curves were hardly noticeable. The buildings not along the road were sometimes visible and most times only the drive was any sign of them. The occasional fence property had a name of the ranch on a wooden sign above the drive.

Joe recognized all the named ranches. He did not necessarily know who lived out this direction, but Joe knew the ranchers more from when they came to drink at the saloon than from anything else. It meant he did not know much about their property, aside from what they were willing to tell him over a drink. Many assumed his knowledge of their ranch and its location, which never bothered him because he did not need the information. Now he was learning some locations at least.

"Does that mean you would never think of getting married?" Broddy asked, "Like if Scarlett decided she was tired of running around."

"I know Scarlett's kind too well to believe her if she claimed to want to settle down and get married," Joe answered, "If I get married it has to be about love and not what I can do for her or what she could do for me."

"I'm surprised at you having such a romantic notion about marriage," Broddy said.

"Why?" Joe asked.

"Because you seem more like the type who prefers getting something out of a relationship," Broddy answered, "The idea you would marry for love is such a strange one."

"When you marry, won't it be for love?" Joe asked, "Why shouldn't I have love too?"

"I see nothing against it," Broddy answered, "Just hard to wrap my mind around it."

"How far out is this outlaw hideout?" Joe asked.

"We still have a while to go," Broddy answered, "I brought enough lunch for both of us."

"It wasn't the meal that was on my mind," Joe said.

"Then what is it?" Broddy asked, "You already said you were fine walking into an outlaw's hideout."

"It isn't about walking into an outlaw's hideout," Joe answered, "It is about riding in."

"Riding?"

"I don't ride much because I usually spend my time dealing with my business, which is in the same building I live in."

Broddy was quiet as he connected what Joe said to what Joe meant. Then he tried to not to laugh, but snorted anyway.

"I understand that pain," Broddy said once he had gotten himself under control.

"Isn't going to help me later," Joe said.

"No, it doesn't," Broddy said.

A cloud of dust came into view. It went over the road as well as on either side. It was hard to see what was causing the cloud until Joe and the sheriff got closer. Then they could see the cattle moving as well as the cowboys sitting on horses on the road on either side. When Joe and Broddy got close enough, they stopped to wait for the cattle to finish. The closest cowboy nodded to them. It would have been impossible to hear anything over the sounds of the cattle, so they sat on their horses without speaking.

Joe didn't know how long the cattle had been moving across the road before he and Broddy arrived, but at least a couple hundred must have gone by while they were waiting. The dust kicked up by the animals was bad enough that Joe found himself sneezing several times. Once the cattle were passed and the cowboys had followed them, the sheriff waited until the dust had calmed down before starting forward. Joe waited without impatience as his nose was already going to take a while to settle.

"The summer has been too dry," Broddy said, "We needed more water to avoid such clouds."

"So, people have been complaining about them," Joe said.

"I guess you hear about such problems as much as I do," Broddy said.

"People tell me all sorts of things while they drink," Joe said, "Complaining about their problems tends to be a favourite, along with commiserating with each other over such matters."

"People want to know they aren't alone," Broddy said.

"And they like to drink about their problems," Joe said, "Why do you think saloons are so profitable?"

"I am just glad it was you who bought the saloon from Pierce," Broddy said, "I was worried that the person who bought it would let things stay as they were, which was why I told Pierce he had to leave town."

"It did take several people a couple visits before they realized I wasn't going to accept violence in the place," Joe said, "But it has been six years and everyone knows the rules now. Aside from Matt and Michael doing their thing, but they have agreed to fix anything they break."

"At least with them, you know one isn't going to show back up with a gun to shoot the place up," Broddy said.

"For all I know they could continue bashing at each other once they are kicked out for the night," Joe said, "But they seem to be fine the next time they are seen. I thought they were brothers for a while, but someone told me they weren't."

"They are brothers-in-law," Broddy said, "And they both work the same ranch, which is owned by Matt's family. I think when they come into town to drink is the only time they get a chance to let off steam."

"That explains why they don't do more damage to each other," Joe said, "Because if they did, they would have to explain the bruises."

"Makes better entertainment when the participants don't get hurt," Broddy said.

"I would prefer if they did less damage to the furniture," Joe said, "They do fix the ones they damage, but those ones are more likely to break again and when someone else is using them."

"You have to discuss the matter with them," Broddy said, "You are the one who allows them to fight in the saloon."

"I could tell them to take their arguments somewhere else," Joe said, "Then you can deal with them."

Broddy didn't respond verbally, but he frowned. Joe didn't offer up anything else. They rode without speaking for a long while. After a while, the fences ran out and there stopped being green grass. The grass Joe could see was much longer and had gone brown. Mixed in were bushes and the occasional tree. The land itself had more hills and there were large rocky outcroppings that came into view.

Joe figured they must have passed all the ranches now and they were into what could be considered the wild. The road still continued as it would because the stagecoach made sure it would never be overgrown or erased. Since the closest town was most of a full day's stagecoach ride, keeping the road clear was a good thing.

The further they went along the road the more groups of rocks came into view. In the distance to the right some hills came into view. It got bigger the more they rode. But it was not the gentle rolling hills, instead was rocky cliffs. There were paths leading up looked narrow and hard to navigate.

Broddy moved off the road and towards the cliffs. Joe let Journey follow along. More dust was created by their passage as this part of the landscape was not as packed as the road. It once again started tickling at Joe's nose. After the first couple sneezes and a coughing fit, Joe pulled his handkerchief over his mouth and nose. He looked with distaste at his clothing but there was little he could do about it and, at least, dust was fairly easy to clean off.

The cliffs got closer and closer. Joe looked them over and he could not see any signs of human inhabitants. The paths going through were natural spaces and had no trace of tracks along them. Likely they had been covered over by the wind blowing the dust around. They reached the base of the cliffs and stopped. The sheriff got down off his horse.

"Might as well stop and have lunch," Broddy said.

"Sure," Joe said after pulling the handkerchief down. He looked at the dirt below the horse. It didn't look like it had a lot of give to it. With a sigh, he swung one leg over the saddle and lowered it to the ground using his arms. The knee gave out as soon as he let some weight on it. This caused him to fall on his backside into the dirt with the other foot still caught in the stirrup.

Journey snorted but did not move. The sheriff had sat

down on a rock with a bag in his hands. With as much of his dignity as he had left, Joe lifted his foot and dislodged it from the stirrup. The boot caused a cloud of dust as he let it drop to the ground.

"You gonna be able to get up?" Broddy asked.

"Give me a minute," Joe answered.

"Okay," Broddy said. He took a sandwich out of the bag and started to eat it. Joe was careful and slow as he tried to get to his feet. His knees did not want to hold him up at first, but he managed to hold onto his horse to keep his balance until he could walk again. When he let go and walked over to where Broddy was, he could feel that he was bow legged but there was nothing he could do about it. Joe reached the rock near Broddy and found it flat enough for him to sit down on. He was still careful not to collapse onto the rock but instead lower himself on it.

"Sandwich?" Broddy asked offering one from the bag.

"Sure," Joe answered. He reached out and took the food. Taking a bite, Joe chewed without tasting any of it. There was enough moisture to keep it from drying out his mouth further. The sandwich was almost gone before Joe realized there was cooked pork inside it.

"You gonna make it back up on your horse?" Broddy asked.

"I can't walk far enough to get back to town today," Joe answered, "And I definitely won't be able to carry on, so I better be able to get back up there."

"Another sandwich?" Broddy asked.

"Yes," Joe answered.

Broddy pulled out two more sandwiches and gave one to Joe, who accepted it and starting to eat.

"Miss. Modahl?" Joe asked.

"What?" Broddy asked.

"Miss. Modahl made the sandwiches?" Joe asked.

"Yes," Broddy answered, "I mentioned yesterday at supper that we were going out for the ride today and she showed up this morning with the food."

"That is nice of her," Joe said.

"I didn't tell her why the ride or that anyone was going to come with me," Broddy said, "But she packed enough for multiple anyway."

"She may have figured you wouldn't go on a long ride without someone else along," Joe said.

"I suppose," Broddy said.

"Or she figured you needed a lot to keep you going," Joe said.

"How long will it take you to be ready to keep going?" Broddy asked.

"A minute or two," Joe answered.

Once they were both finished the sandwiches, Broddy got up and went to his horse. He put the bag back in the saddle bag before turning back to Joe. He made no move, just stood and watching. Joe did not try to move for another minute. When he did, he used his arms to lift himself off the rock. His knees still were not sure about holding his weight, but they did not give out as before. He still walked bow legged to his horse.

Joe used his arms to get high enough he could swing his leg around and get on the saddle properly. Once he was settled. Joe looked over and saw Broddy was already on his horse and waiting.

"Let's go," Joe said.

Broddy nodded before directed his horse along the closest path. The path was barely wide enough for Broddy and his horse, so Joe followed along behind him. The path made a turn to the left and then immediately started up a slope. It was fairly steep. The horses slowed as they worked to keep their footing. The rocks on either side crowded the path. Joe noticed Broddy was watching for anyone who could be above then, but Joe did not see anyone when he glanced up there.

The path curved around a larger rock and leveled out until

they reached the other side. Then it went up again. They came out at the top of one of the rocks. Joe looked behind him and saw the dusty landscape they had left behind. The path headed downward in between some more rocks. In only a few steps, they went from lots of space to another narrow path. There was barely even room to go around the occasional bush that grew along it. Fortunately, the bushes were small due to not enough light so the horses had an easy time in stepping over them.

When they reached another leveling out of the path, they stayed along it as they went around large rock walls. It was dark as the sunlight did not get that far down, however it was enough to see by. The bushes were no longer a problem. The path had actually widened a little bit, but not enough to ride abreast.

"This is made by water," Joe said.

"Really?" Broddy asked.

"Yeah, water carved this space in the rocks," Joe said, "They probably fill with water when it rains."

"Fortunately, it is a cloudless day," Broddy said.

"Makes it harder to get the outlaws," Joe said.

"Likely why they chose to live here," Broddy said.

"Makes sense to me," Joe said.

Broddy had been checking above them in case someone was up there, now Joe noticed Broddy looking straight up on occasion to make sure no clouds had shown up.

The path went down for a short bit and then back up for another bit before leveling off again. This happened a few times as the path curved around going both left and right. The rocks walls were towering over them as they went.

"It would be easy to get lost in here," Broddy said.

"This is just a small area with only one path," Joe said, "I've heard of bigger areas with far more paths. It is supposed to be beautiful to see."

"Sounds like a death trap," Broddy said, "The beauty sucks

you in, then you lose your way, and finally nature takes you out."

"Might be an interesting place to explore," Joe said, "If the proper precautions are taken."

"What are the proper precautions to walking into a death trap?" Broddy asked.

"Knowledge," Joe answered, "Getting to know the situation, such as the terrain, weather patterns, edible plants, and water sources. Then packing for what could happen, but assuming the items won't last."

"You have done such things before?" Broddy asked.

"You asked me how to prepare to enter a death trap," Joe answered.

"Does it work?" Broddy asked.

"Depends on the death trap," Joe answered, "Also on what information is available, because without good information the preparation is useless."

"I think I'll leave you to wander death traps and skip things myself," Broddy said, "It is bad enough to walk into an outlaw's hideout though this path."

The path started climbing again, only this time it did not switch to downward after a short period. Instead it got steeper. Then the path went close to vertical. Joe was worried they were going to have to get down and walk, but it never got bad enough. As he was not sure he could have walked, Joe was glad they could stay on their horses.

At the top of the path were two boulders with barely enough room between them for a horse and rider. Joe thought he saw movement around the left boulder, but when he looked again there was nothing. However, Broddy came alert, so he must have seen the movement as well. Neither man made any move for their guns. Guns were not likely to do them good as this point anyway as their opponents had the higher ground as well as the direction of the sun.

Joe followed right behind Broddy so there was limited

space for causing trouble. The space on the other side of the boulders was a plateau with brush and another path going farther up. Also were four men on horses with rifles pointed at Joe and Broddy, who had stopped once they had seen the guns.

"We would like to talk to Slick," Sheriff Broddy said.

"What if Slick doesn't want to talk to you?" the man on the right asked.

"Well, why don't you ask him rather determining that for him?" Sheriff Broddy asked.

"He is on his way," the man said.

"Good," Sheriff Broddy said.

Everyone was quiet as they waited. There was some communication between the man who spoke and the one next to him, even though they didn't speak. The wind blew across the plateau, but they were high enough there was no dust in it. Instead there was a sweet scent Joe enjoyed but could not identify.

Movement came from the path above them. Joe looked up to see a man riding down towards them. Joe recognized Slick McQueen, without having met the man before. As Slick's horse moved, Joe could see silver studs on Slick's clothing shining when the sun hit them. When Slick reached the plateau, he stopped behind the man who had been the speaker.

"What can I do for you, Sheriff?" Slick asked.

"I was hoping we could talk," Sheriff Broddy answered.

"We are both here," Slick said, "What do you want to talk about?"

"Len Grady was murdered this week," Sheriff Broddy said.

"That is sad news," Slick said with a slight tilt of his head.

"He was home a day earlier than he was supposed to be," Sheriff Broddy said.

"You are pretty far from town to bring out such news," Slick said. His head straightened when he started speaking and then tilted back as he finished.

"I would hardly make the ride out if there wasn't a reason," Sheriff Broddy said.

"I have no choice but to be suspicious of your motives," Slick said, "I have a warrant out for my arrest." The tilted happened again like strange twitch.

"And this is too far out of my territory for me to arrest you," Sheriff Broddy said, "However, I was told that you were seen at the Grady's place the day Len was killed."

Slick looked surprised. The man, who had spoken earlier, turned to looked at Slick, but the rest kept their eyes on Broddy and Joe.

"Who would say such a thing?" Slick asked. His head didn't straighten this time, it stay tilted.

"I would prefer not to say," Sheriff Broddy answered, "As I don't need another body to stick in the ground, or any other trouble in town."

"You said talk," Slick said, "If Len is dead and you allege I was there, shouldn't you be here to arrest me?"

"I don't know if you are the murderer," Sheriff Broddy answered, "And I don't want to accuse anyone until I have more information. I don't know if you were at the Grady place at the same time as Len's murderer. I only know you were there."

"Are you expecting me to admit to you whether I was there?" Slick asked.

"Actually, we found that two people left the Grady place in a hurry," Sheriff Broddy answered, "And we have had trouble locating Len's wife since his body was discovered. I was hoping you would be willing to admit to knowing her location."

"You are accusing me of kidnapping instead?" Slick asked. His eyes narrowed along with the head tilt.

"I am not accusing you of anything," Sheriff Broddy answered, "I am not foolish enough to come out to your territory and accuse you in this matter. In fact, all I want to know is if you have knowledge of Mrs. Grady's whereabouts."

"And if I do?" Slick asked.

"We would like to talk to her about her husband's death," Sheriff Broddy answered.

"Why?" Slick asked.

"We believe she was there at the time of the murder," Broddy answered, "Also we would like to know that she is safe."

Slick tilted his head a little further as he thought about his answer. The man in front of him looked back also waiting for the response. Even the other men shifted slightly as they waited.

"I know Mrs. Grady's location," Slick said, "She is safe."

"Is it possible for us to speak with her?" Sheriff Broddy asked.

"Not at this moment," Slick answered.

"Would it be possible to speak with her before we leave?" Sheriff Broddy asked.

"It may be possible," Slick answered.

He was quiet as he thought about it a bit more. Everyone waited for anything further. Joe thought he might have noticed the actual movement of the sun while Slick thought it out.

"Wait here," Slick said before signalling to his men. He turned and headed back up the path. Three of the men followed him up. The last man settled himself on his horse in expectation of being there a while. He also put his rifle into a resting position instead of a shooting one.

Joe swung his leg off the saddle and used his arms to lower himself to the ground.

"What are you doing?" Broddy asked. The tone suggested curiousity rather than nervousness.

"Stretching my legs," Joe answered, "Otherwise, I'm not sure about moving later." His legs wanted to give out again, but he managed to stay on his feet. The man on guard duty watching them but did not move. Joe did what he could to stay on his feet as he stretched out his legs. It was slow but after a while Joe could actually let go and not collapse. He walked around a little bit and looked bow legged as he did so.

The man who was guarding them smirked as Joe's activity, but Joe was too concerned about getting his mobility back to worry about it. Broddy was spending his time looking out at the view. After a while, Broddy got down and wandered to the edge to look down. The man guarding them relaxed a bit more as neither Joe nor Broddy appeared to have any interest in trying to go farther.

Joe was just about able to walk upright and Broddy was squatted down at the edge, when they heard a horse coming down the path. They looked up to see Slick coming back and Mrs. Grady behind him in the saddle. Broddy went over to stand by his horse. Joe did the same. When Slick got close enough, he stopped his horse. He got down before helping Mrs. Grady do the same.

"You wanted to talk to me?" Mrs. Grady asked Broddy.

"I did, Ma'am," Sheriff Broddy answered, "I would like to start out by saying that it is good to see you in good health. When we couldn't find you after your husband's body was found, it worried us."

"McQueen has been nice enough to provide me with a safe place," Mrs. Grady said.

"Then you were at home when your husband arrived home," Sheriff Broddy said.

"I was," Mrs. Grady said.

"Was he with someone else?" Sheriff Broddy asked.

"I didn't see him," Mrs. Grady answered, "I didn't see anyone."

"What did you hear?" Sheriff Broddy asked.

"There were two horses," Mrs. Grady answered, "They were talking as they got down and came towards the house, but I couldn't identify the second man. Then Len cried out. I was frozen until the other person tried the door and then I hurried to the back of the house in fear for my life."

"Did you see the person when you rode away?" Sheriff Broddy asked.

"No," Mrs. Grady answered, "They must have left as soon as they found the door locked."

"What about Len's horse?" Sheriff Broddy asked.

"I don't remember," Mrs. Grady answered.

"It wasn't there," Slick said, "Neither horse was."

Mrs. Grady glanced back at Slick as if he said the wrong thing, but he just shrugged. Broddy ignored both the look and the response.

"You think the person thinks you saw them?" Sheriff Broddy asked.

"I don't know," Mrs. Grady answered, "But I am worried he could come after me next."

"I can understand that worry," Sheriff Broddy said, "And I'm not going to ask you to go anywhere you don't feel safe."

"Are you actually going to catch the murderer?" Mrs. Grady asked.

"I am going to do my best," Sheriff Broddy answered.

"What about my husband's body?" Mrs. Grady asked.

"I asked Doc McKaig to put him in the grave," Sheriff Broddy answered, "I figured the gravestone could be figured out when you were found and tell us what should go on it."

Mrs. Grady nodded as she bit her lip.

"Whenever you are ready," Sheriff Broddy said, "For now the grave is marked so we know where he is. The property is also going to wait until you are ready."

"Thank you," Mrs. Grady said.

"What happens if you don't catch the murderer and she isn't ever safe going back into town?" Slick asked.

"I will figure something out to make sure Mrs. Grady can deal with those matters," Sheriff Broddy answered, "I will need them taken care of anyway as having a property without the owner around can bring trouble."

Slick nodded in understanding.

"Do you have any more questions?" Mrs. Grady asked.

"I believe that is it," Sheriff Broddy answered, "And I am sorry for your loss."

Mrs. Grady nodded before turning around. Slick helped her back on to the horse before getting up into the saddle. They headed back up the path. When they passed the man on guard duty, he straightened up and brought the rifle back to firing position.

"Let's go before we wear out our welcome," Broddy said as he pulled himself into the saddle.

"I think that is a very close deadline," Joe said as he did the same.

They got the horses turned around and Joe followed Broddy through the boulders. They headed down the path without talking. It was just as steep going down as it had been going up. Joe knew that he could have gotten down and walked if he had to, but since they had not gotten down to come up, he was not as worried going down. It did get steep enough in places Joe was not sure that they were not going to have to walk.

Finally they reached the bottom, where they were surrounded by the towering rock walls. Joe moved in closer to Broddy but was still riding behind him. He noticed that now they were in there, Broddy was back to checking the sky to make sure no clouds have appeared in the time since they were through the last time.

"So, what now?" Joe asked.

"As far as the case?" Broddy said, "I need to figure out what happened to Len's horse."

"Why not just go around asking if you are allowed to check people's barns?" Joe asked.

"And when they refuse?" Broddy asked.

"Most people wouldn't," Joe answered, "And those who do are suspects."

"There are a few around who seem like they would, but they really won't," Broddy said, "It has nothing to do with being connected to the murder and just they don't like letting anyone in a position of authority into their property."

"I suppose they could cause some problems," Joe said, "Though it is pretty easy to identify them over someone who is trying to hide something."

"Also if I start going through one barn, by the time I finish with it the rest of the town knows what is going on," Broddy said, "Most won't understand why, but the one who is hiding the horse will make sure I don't find it in their barn."

"I guess that won't work," Joe said, "But there has to be some way to move forward with the investigation from here."

"Right now, I am hoping to get back to town without incident," Broddy said, "And then tomorrow refocus on the investigation. Sometimes things come up when no one is looking."

"You will have to tell McPherson that Mrs. Grady has been found," Joe said.

"That will be the easy part," Broddy said.

"He will want to know more than just that she is found and she is safe," Joe said, "He always wants to know the whole story."

"I am sure he will," Broddy said, "But unless you are going to start running your mouth, which would take a change in personality, McPherson isn't going to get the story."

"As much as he would have fun with the story of us going to Slick McQueen's hideout, I don't think he needs to know," Joe said.

"Is there ever a story he needs to know?" Broddy asked.

"Probably somewhere," Joe answered.

Broddy chuckled. They fell into that comfortable companionship that did not need conversation as they continued through the ravine. This went on when they reached the path going up and down through the rocks. When they exited the rocks, they stopped. But they didn't talk as they rested. Joe got down and walked around in an effort to avoid getting too cramped. Again he was bow legged when he got down, but by the time Broddy was ready to go Joe was walking straighter.

As they continued on, Joe put the handkerchief over his nose and mouth to keep from breathing in too much dust. Since it was desert, the horses kicked up dust as they went. Only once they reached the road did it died down enough that Joe could breathe without the handkerchief. The sun had been slowly moving towards the horizon once they had gotten out of the rocks and it disappeared as they reached the edge of the ranchland. Lights along the road came from houses, but sometimes the only thing that could be seen was that there was light and not the buildings.

"It is going to be late when we get back," Broddy said.

"Still hours before closing time," Joe said.

"You gonna stay up to see closing time?" Broddy asked.

"Probably not tonight," Joe answered, "I was up far earlier than I usually see and it has been a long ride. I can trust Jake to close up with the help of Miss. Edwards."

"Since the game ended last night, there is no worry about DeWhite not leaving," Broddy said.

"Not unless he found someone new to play," Joe said, "But the stagecoach was not due today, so I doubt there is anyone new in town who would be interested in playing. Most professional players don't ride in."

"I never noticed that, but you are right," Broddy said, "They usually come by stagecoach."

"When your business depends on it, you notice these things," Joe said.

"I just know the stagecoach schedule," Broddy said, "And watch out for those who ride in."

"And that is your business," Joe said.

"I suppose it is," Broddy said.

They fell back into not speaking as they traveled.

When they reached town, they said good night before going their separate ways. Joe headed for the stable. William was there and took Journey from Joe, who was not as bow legged when he got down as he had been worried he would be. He walked back to the saloon. It was at the usual level of activity. DeWhite was in his seat at the table with Miss. Karina at his side and Shorty behind him.

Seated at the bar were Henczel and McPherson. They looked at Joe as he walked over to the bar. He signalled Jake to get him a drink. As he sat down in his seat, Jake gave him the drink.

"What happened to you?" McPherson asked, "I didn't think you could get that dirty and survive."

"It is just dirt," Joe answered, "It will come out in the laundry."

"We asked Jake where you went, but he didn't know," McPherson said.

"I went with the sheriff in search of Mrs. Grady," Joe said.

"And?" McPherson asked.

"She is safe," Joe answered.

"And?" McPherson asked.

"I don't think it is my place to give you any more information," Joe said.

"But you went with him," McPherson said, "You could give more information."

"I think I gave you all that I can," Joe said.

"The lady, who doesn't work here, came down and was looking for you," Henczel said.

"I am sure she did," Joe said.

"But she went back upstairs when she was told you weren't around," Henczel said.

"I doubt she will leave before tomorrow," Joe said.

"She likely wouldn't," Henczel said, "The stagecoach does leave tomorrow morning, but since she hasn't taken it out of here yet it seems unlikely she will take that one."

"Not sure why she is still around," Joe said, "But I doubt she has achieved it yet."

"She wants you," Henczel said.

"That isn't what I am not sure about," Joe said, "It is which part she wants that I am not sure about. She isn't going to be staying on a more permanent basis."

"Money tends to be popular among her kind," Henczel said.

"Then she will be leaving without anything she wants," Joe said, "Because I don't plan on parting with any of my money without getting a product or service of equal value in return."

"Well, the rest of the ladies who stay in your saloon tend to exchange sex as a service," Henczel said, "I wouldn't be surprised if she has done the same at a previous time."

"If that is what she wanted, she would have come in with that offer," Joe said, "And she didn't. She also hasn't gone up with anyone."

"True," Henczel said, "She has turned down offers by several men. Maybe she just wants someone to warm her bed for a while but not in a paid for it kind of way."

"Likely I will find out the longer she stays," Joe said, "But not tonight."

"You could probably knock on her door and find out if she is still awake," Henczel said.

"Not tonight," Joe said.

"Are we keeping you up?" McPherson asked.

"Yes," Joe answered, "But so am I."

"It must have been an interesting day," McPherson said.

"Well, it was long," Joe said, "Not sure about interesting."

"Really?" McPherson asked, "What made it long?"

"The length," Joe answered, "Did you know that the sun comes up during the time referred to as the morning?"

"I've been made aware of the matter, yes," McPherson answered.

"The mornings are not my thing," Joe said.

"You didn't know that before?" Henczel asked.

"I thought I did," Joe answered, "But I must have forgotten as I got up during that time today and have been up since then."

"Perhaps you should find a way to get up the stairs to where you can locate a bed," Henczel said, "McPherson can grill you in the morning to see if you will give up more then."

"Good idea," Joe said. He finished his drink before getting up. Each muscle in his legs screamed in protest, but he managed to stay on his feet without looking too stiff. Joe made his way to the stairs. He knew it looked strange but he moved slowly up the stairs.

As much as he would like to have asked for a bath to be drawn, Joe was not going to request that of Miss. Edwards at this point in the evening. Instead he stripped off his clothes where the dirt was contained and then washed up before crawling into bed.


Sheriff Broddy entered his office by the back door because he was coming from the stable. His deputy was sitting beside the stove with a cup of coffee in his hand. In Broddy's own chair was Amy Modahl.

"Good evening, ma'am," Broddy said as he removed his hat, "What can I help you with?"

"I brought you supper," Miss. Modahl answered, "But I was told you had not returned yet."

"Unfortunately, my journey took the whole day," Broddy said.

"Did you find what you were looking for?" Miss. Modahl asked.

"I did," Broddy answered, "My journey today was to see if I could find Mrs. Grady and it was a success. She is safe, but she will not be returning for now."

"What is going to happen to the Grady's property?" the deputy asked.

"Nothing for right now," Broddy answered, "I told her nothing would happen with anything until she is able to get back to town and have a say in the matter."

"But for how long?" the deputy asked.

"As long as we can," Broddy answered.

"I'll go wander the town," the deputy said as he got up. He put the cup on the top of the stove and then went out front door. Broddy dragged the chair over to the desk and sat down.

"Your sandwiches were enjoyed, so thank you for them," Broddy said.

"You're welcome," Miss. Modahl said, "Are you sure Mrs. Grady is safe?"

"Yes," Broddy answered, "If it was any other situation, I would have worries about it but she is safe."

"Good," Miss. Modahl said, "I was starting to worry about her. Oh, yes, your supper." She got to her feet and went to the stove. Opening it, she took out a metal tray and brought it over to the desk. She set it down in front of Broddy.

"Thank you," Broddy said as he took the cutlery that were already waiting on the desk and started eating. Miss. Modahl sat back down in the chair.

"Your deputy was concerned about wherever you went and the fact that you took Joe McGraw with you as back up," Miss. Modahl said.

"I know," Broddy said, "But he was needed here and McGraw has been helping me with this matter making it easier for him to back me up today. My deputy doesn't trust McGraw."

"I haven't had much contact with him," Miss. Modahl said, "But he doesn't seem like a bad person."

"He doesn't talk about himself much," Broddy said, "I don't have a problem with him. Unlike the previous owner of the saloon, McGraw prefers to keep the violence out."

"I would prefer if he didn't keep ladies in the upper rooms,"

Miss. Modahl said, "But I have talked to a couple and know that he doesn't force any of them to work. He only rents the rooms to them. There was one lady he actually sent out to Laine's Place due to him feeling she shouldn't be working."

"That was nice of him," Broddy said, "It isn't a solution to the problem, but it is a small piece. Unfortunately, there are men who look for that service and that is hard to change."

"Have you gone into the saloon looking for a lady?" Miss. Modahl asked.

"No," Broddy answered. He looked her in the eyes, so she could see he was telling the truth. She nodded and smiled a little.

"It is late," Broddy said, "Would you like me to take you home when I am finished eating?"

"After you have been riding all-day?" Miss. Modahl asked, "It might be best if I stay in town for the night. I am not needed out at Laine's Place tonight."

"You can stay at my place for the night," Broddy said, "I'll be here in my office."

"Are you sure?" Miss. Modahl asked, "I can ask someone else for a place to stay."

"I am sure," Broddy nodded.

"Thank you," Miss. Modahl said.

"The least I can do for such a good supper," Broddy said.

Before either could say anything else, the door opened and the deputy stepped inside. He looked like he had been running.

# Chapter Five
## The Mayor

When Joe came down the stairs the next morning, he found McPherson and Henczel sitting at the bar drinking. Instead of appearing to be ready to start asking questions, they were morose. Jake was behind the bar serving them. Joe went over and sat down in his usual seat. Jake poured another drink and pushed it over to Joe.

"What happened?" Joe asked.

"Mr. Cheshire, the mayor, died last night," McPherson answered, "Miss. Rachelle, his housekeeper, found him late last night. It is believed that he died in his sleep."

"He must have been doing worse than he allowed people to think," Joe said.

"I know he was losing it mentally," Henczel said, "But he seemed good otherwise. I visited him yesterday and we talked over coffee. He gave no sign of being ill."

"Maybe we have a murderer among us," McPherson said.

"I doubt anyone killed the mayor," Joe said, "No one wanted the position, except Henczel."

"You did say you had coffee with him yesterday," McPherson said turning to Henczel.

"I told you that I wasn't in a hurry to get the position," Henczel said, "I wouldn't kill for it."

"Maybe you did it out of pity," McPherson said, "You knew he was losing it mentally and you didn't want him embarrassing himself at a council meeting."

"I don't think that was the issue," Joe said, "The mayor said some pretty embarrassing things without Henczel correcting the matter and you should know because you printed them."

"I don't remember everything I have printed," McPherson said, "I have printed hundreds of articles since I started the paper here, I can't remember all of it."

"Doesn't matter," Henczel said, "I didn't kill him."

"Henczel gains nothing from the mayor's death," Joe said, "And I doubt pity would direct his actions."

"Besides he died in his sleep, not while we were having coffee," Henczel said.

"That is the perfect way to administer slow acting poison," McPherson said, "You could slip it into his coffee and it wouldn't take effect until later in the day,"

"And where did I get this slow acting poison?" Henczel asked, "It doesn't sound like anything Mrs. Gilbert at the general store would sell me."

"You make it out of natural plants," McPherson said, "If you bought it, the poison could be traced back to you. But if you make it then no one would know, except you."

"And which native plants make the most effective slow acting poison?" Henczel asked, "Because I have never studied botany enough to know which ones were edible let alone which were poisonous."

"I don't know," McPherson said, "I have never studied the plants around here either."

"Then how would either of us know if any of the native plants are even poisonous?" Henczel asked.

"I don't think you are going to be able to write a story about Henczel murdering the mayor with a slow acting poison unless you make it up," Joe said, "And that is libel for which you could lose your newspaper if Henczel decided to take you to court. And out of everyone in town, he not only knows how destroy you that way, he would do so."

"Given that the mayor was old and slowing down in the brain, he probably wouldn't be telling people how sick he really was because people would have suggested he step down as mayor," McPherson said.

"Now we are going to have to hold an election anyway," Henczel said, "We should fill the position before the next council meeting."

"Or we could wait until the meeting to see who wants to throw their hats into the ring," McPherson said.

"We should have a meeting about that sooner," Henczel said, "Like in the next few days."

"I am sure that once word gets around a meeting will happen," Joe said, "It tends to happen."

Before McPherson and Henczel could say anything, the door to the saloon opened. All four of the men looked up to see the deputy escorting Miss. Rachelle inside. She had obviously been crying and was still hiccupping. Rather than take her to sit at the bar, the deputy took her to the table nearest the bar. Jake poured a drink and Joe took it to the table. Joe set it in front of Miss. Rachelle. She took a sip to steady herself. The deputy sat down beside her. Joe inquired, without speaking, whether the deputy want a drink. The deputy shook his head. Joe went back to sit at the bar.

It was quiet with only Miss. Rachelle's hiccups interrupting it. Everyone sipped their drinks and tried not to feel uncomfortable. Miss. Edwards came out of the kitchen with a plate of lunch. She delivered it to Joe. She asked if anyone else was hungry but was just met with head shakes. After giving Miss. Rachelle a brief hug, Miss. Edwards went back into the kitchen. Joe found his chewing was loud as the uncomfortable quiet came again. He tried to chew quieter but did not feel very successful.

Joe was just about done his meal, when the door opened. The Gilberts entered followed by the Jarretts. The ladies joined Miss. Rachelle at the table, while the men sat down at the bar. This started conversations to fill the uncomfortable quiet.

When Joe finished his meal, he took the dishes back to the

kitchen. Miss. Edwards was doing make work to keep herself busy.

"Others are arriving," Joe said, "If you wanted to join them."

Miss. Edwards nodded as she took the dishes from him. She took them to the sink, which already has water in it. Joe went back into the main room as she started washing.

More people had arrived while Joe was in the kitchen. All except Henczel had moved from the bar to a table. Joe sat down in his seat.

"A few more and we'll have the whole town council," Henczel said.

"Give it a while," Joe said, "Doc McKaig and Sheriff Broddy will probably be the last to arrive."

"What about the ranchers?" Henczel asked, "Do you think many of them will show up?"

"As word gets out and they get their chores done," Joe said, "Same as last time there was an important death. A few people wanted to bring the coffin in here, but I said no."

"Didn't want your saloon into a funeral home?" Henczel asked.

"Not even temporarily," Joe answered, "Because once the precedent has been set, it is impossible to go back on it. And bodies attract things I don't want to have to get rid of from my saloon."

"I suppose that is understandable," Henczel said, "Though why meet here rather than around the body then?"

"I don't know," Joe answered, "Likely that was how things were long before I arrived."

"The last owner must not have been bothered by having a body in his saloon," Henczel said.

"He didn't mind if people came in and destroyed all his furniture," Joe said, "It is possible that people died in here, so having a dead body sitting in a coffin wouldn't have been much of an issue."

"What happened to him?" Henczel asked.

"Broddy requested he leave town," Joe answered.

"Things must have been pretty bad for that to happen," Henczel said, "Considering how relaxed Broddy is about some things, he must have done something unforgivable."

"His running of this saloon was not the matter that caused Broddy to ask him to leave," Joe said.

"You aren't going to tell me, are you?" Henczel asked.

"I only know half the story," Joe answered, "And I'm pretty sure it is not mine to tell. Broddy might be willing to say more."

"He is more willing to tell than you," Henczel said, "But only if he feels it is something the person should know. You still have him beat on not saying anything."

"What do you expect of me?" Joe asked.

"Usually those in the saloon or tend the bar are willing to tell people things," Henczel answered, "You know the going to the bartender to gain information."

"Jake is the bartender," Joe said.

"You know what I mean," Henczel said.

"I do," Joe said, "But I chose not to spread stories. It doesn't end well when people do."

"Or everyone has a good laugh," Henczel said, "Depending on the story."

The door of the saloon opened and more people came in. These were ranchers and their families. They found tables and joined conversations. A few came over to the bar to get a drink before taking seats. Joe and Henczel did not say anything until things were settled again. It felt right to Joe to start a story, despite his stance not to tell other's stories.

"There was a young man with no worldly experience," Joe said, "He had only two things as he left the home he had known his whole life. One was the horse he was riding on and the other was a pocket watch that his grandfather had brought to this new world years earlier. This young man had no idea the object of his search as his knowledge was limited to not being able to stay."

Joe stopped as a couple people came back to the bar for refills. Henczel watched them as if annoyed by their presence. They stayed near the bar for several minutes talking before taking their drinks back to the tables. Henczel turned back to Joe, who merely sipped his drink as if he had no knowledge of what Henczel was looking for.

"What did he find?" Henczel asked.

"Who?" Joe asked.

"The young man you started telling the story about," Henczel answered.

"Oh, him," Joe said, "It was not really surprising what happened to him. He met a group of men along the road. They were all traveling in the same direction, though the young man didn't really know where he was headed. "

Miss. Edwards came out of the kitchen. She came over to the bar and ordered a drink. Once Jake had poured it, she took it with her to the table with Miss. Rachelle and sat down there. Henczel once again turned back to Joe to hear more of the story.

"Why did he leave?" Jake asked before Henczel could speak up.

"What?" Joe asked.

"You said the young man had the knowledge that he could not stay at his home," Jake answered, "Why couldn't he stay?"

"There was nothing there for him," Joe answered, "His family had too many members for the amount of resources available. It wouldn't have mattered how much work he did for the family, he would have starved anyway. He was the young male of the family and they made a priority to feed the children and the parents of those children."

"It would hardly be the first family who were forced to choose who got to eat," Henczel said, "But it is a hard choice to make."

"Rather than stay and starve the young man left to find his own way," Joe said.

"So, he met some men on the road," Henczel said.

"He did," Joe said, "They learned that he was a naïve and inexperienced traveller. He didn't learn anything about them, not even their names. Unfortunately, he was too inexperienced to understand that was a bad thing and there was a warning in it. Even when he woke up bloody and broken beside the road, the young man didn't fully understand what happened."

"He was lucky they left him alive," Henczel said, "So many aren't."

"I doubt they cared," Joe said, "They likely just hit him over the head and beat him without worrying about whether he survived it or not."

"That is where luck comes in," Henczel said, "His luck."

"Finding himself in a ditch can't be the end of the story," Jake said, "Because otherwise it would be a warning, not a story."

"It is not the end of the story," Joe said, "The young man survived the beating."

"Some friendly passerby helped him?" Henczel asked.

"No," Joe answered, "He crawled. Using his unbroken leg and good arm, he crawled. Over sharp sticks, hard rocks, baked ground, grass stubble, and around bushes, he crawled. He couldn't tell how long it was that he crawled. It was possible that he blacked out several times from both exertion and pain. Even years later, he could not tell how long he crawled in the dirt or how far he went."

"And no one helped him?" Henczel asked, "Didn't someone pass by?"

"The young man had no memory of anyone going passed him," Joe answered, "It may be because no one went by, or it could be that anyone going by thought he was dead. Not being there, it is hard to tell what happened and the young man was in no condition to give a full account of that time."

"I suppose being that close to death would cause things to be missed," Henczel said.

"That much pain tends to dull a person's perception," Joe said.

"Speaking from experience?" Henczel asked.

"Not going to answer that," Joe answered.

"What about the young man?" Jake asked, "If he told you his story, he must have found some help from somewhere."

"He did," Joe answered, "He came across a cabin, where a settler and his wife were living. They took him in and helped bandage his wounds. Without having much, they shared what they could and gave him space to recover. He did what he could to help them out, but there was little he could actual do until some of the bones that had been broken healed. As much as he wanted to do more, the young man found it best to leave once he was able as they didn't have much extra to give him. This time he was less naïve, horseless, and still without any idea of where to go."

More people came up to the bar for a refill. Jake did his job as Henczel waited impatiently for Joe to continue. Those at the nearest table had stopped talking to each other and had started listening to Joe. They also showed some impatience at the interruption. Joe ignored it all as he took a sip of his drink. Those who came over for refills went back to their table. Henczel waited a moment longer, but Joe gave no sign of continuing.

"The young man must have found what he was looking for," Henczel said, "Which was likely a place where he could stay and still eat."

"Would it matter if he did?" Joe asked.

"I want to know what the place he was looking for was like," Henczel answered, "And I can't know if you don't finish telling his story."

"I can tell you he found what he was looking for," Joe said.

"But there is a story in how he got there," Henczel said, "And I want to hear it. You started to tell the young man's story, you can't give up now."

"I can," Joe said, "Just because you want to hear the rest of it doesn't mean I have to tell it."

"It hardly fair to start telling a story if you didn't plan on finishing it," Jake said.

"The young man managed to reach the next town," Joe said, "But it didn't help because he had nothing. The only thing he had left from the attack was ripped clothing and the settlers merely helped him patch it. In town everything cost something and he couldn't afford any of it. There was no food or shelter he could find for himself. Due to his appearance, the young man found businesses asking him to find other places to be."

"Must have been back east," one of the men from the table commented, "Us out west know not to judge a man by his clothes."

There were nods of agreement from the rest sitting at the table. Joe took another sip from his drink. Henczel glared at the men at the table for their interruption.

"I was never told much about the town," Joe said, "So, I don't know the placement or the people. All I know is the young man didn't fit in and he had some difficulties while there. It was the second day of him being there when he found a job helping clean out the stables. Though it was likely the owner took pity on him than help was actually needed. It was, however, enough for the young man to get some food before he starved and provided him with some space in the stable to sleep; both being more than he entered the town with."

"But it isn't what he was searching for," Henczel said.

"It was more than he had at his home," Joe said, "The job cleaning out the stables was enough for the young man as he earned enough to eat and spent much of his time out of the elements. The owner was willing to keep him around as it meant someone else would do the dirty work."

"You aren't trying to end the story here, are you?" Henczel asked.

"No," Joe answered, "I am telling it as I was told it. For several months, the young man didn't see any point in trying for anything better because it was an improvement over where he had been so far in life. It was while he was working in the horse apples and straw that he saw the owners of the horses and what they had, that the young man started to see a life beyond the smell of his current position. The men had money, power, and respect."

"You don't get those shoveling-" the man's comment was interrupted by the door to the saloon opening and more people coming in. It was more ranchers and their families. They settled in quickly with a few coming to get drinks.

"He wouldn't be making enough money to get anywhere close to the men he was admiring," Henczel said.

"All the money he was making was going into feeding him," Joe said, "He could not get any other jobs that might help him make anything extra because no one wanted him close enough that they could smell him. Only the few times when he managed to get himself cleaned up enough in the river could he run errands or do other small jobs for people. But he could not it as often as he liked due to work and the river."

This time when Joe stopped because a couple men came to the bar to get refills, three tables were annoyed as they had all quit talking and were listening to the story. Joe sipped his drink and waited. Henczel had relaxed some and did the same. Jake finished pouring the drinks and the men moved back to their table.

"Even doing errands he wouldn't have been making much," Henczel said.

"The young man had been there for a month or two when a couple of men rode into town," Joe said, "This wouldn't have meant much to him as many people came through and left their horses in the stable. The young man had never seen either man before, but he recognized the one man's horse as the horse that had been stolen from him by the group of men who had left him for dead. It was even his saddle still on the horse."

"They really must have thought he was dead if they didn't go very far to sell his horse," Henczel said, "But was there any proof this was his horse?"

"He had none and he had not reported the attack," Joe answered, "There was nothing to show this was his horse. The horse was affectionate towards him, but most of the horses were friendly with him so it was hardly any indication of ownership."

"He couldn't have left things alone," Henczel said, "That was his horse. What about the town's sheriff?"

"He never said whether he talked to the sheriff or not," Joe said, "I don't know who he talked to about the situation or what solutions he looked into. I only know what he told me he did. Once darkness fell, the young man put the saddle back on the horse and rode him out of town. Back on the road, he went through the night in attempt to get as far from that town as possible so when it was discovered the horse was gone it would be harder to find him. It must have worked because he never saw anyone after him."

"I guess stealing back your own horse is one way to get it back," Henczel said, "But tends to come back later in life."

"What about the pocket watch?" Jake asked.

"The young man didn't see it with either man," Joe answered, "He didn't know what happened to the pocket watch."

"That leaves him on the run," Henczel said, "He is still looking for his own place in the world and he doesn't have any money to help him."

"It didn't sound like the end of the story," Jake said.

"If you quit interrupting, maybe he can finish the story," one of the men from the closest table said.

"He is going to finish the story whether we interrupt or not," Henczel said, "I am trying to get clarification on things."

The man crossed his arms over his chest and set his mouth into a frown. Henczel turned back to Joe, who took another sip of his drink.

"Since the young man no longer had to walk, he was able to get much farther than he would have otherwise," Joe said, "His few coins would not stretch very far, so if he could he would eat plants or get enough work the people would be willing to feed him. He no longer smelled like stable, but the dirt of the road tended to attach itself to him. More people were willing to work with him as the dirt didn't offend their sensibilities as much. However, the young man didn't find any place he felt was worth staying as many of them he would only find work in similar positions. He told me that little happened during this time as he was more experienced with people and could tell who was more honest, which helped him keep what little he had."

"How long did he travel for?" Henczel asked.

"His guess was about six months," Joe answered, "But it might have been longer as he said he lost track of time for a while as he had limited access to calendars."

"Understandable," Henczel said, "Few of us are good at knowing days while we are traveling. Though sometimes it can be figured out by comparing when they left and the next time a calendar is seen."

"The only issue there is having the knowledge about the date left," Joe said, "If you start out somewhere there is no calendar, but things are figured out by the season, as the young man did, it is a lot harder to know how long the journey was even after finding a calendar."

"I guess it depends on whether the person feels knowing timelines are important," Henczel said, "I rarely lose track

of what day it is, but I have found few others to be the same.
What caused him to stop his journey?"

"He was riding one day when the young man saw a body
lying beside the road," Joe answered, "He stopped to check
and found the man to be still alive. However, he was too
injured to move him. Whoever attacked the man appeared
to have been trying to kill him. The young man did his best
to patch the man up and make him a soft place to rest. The
young man had nothing for supplies, but he got them food
by scavenging and brought water from a nearby river. The
man drifted in and out of consciousness throughout the first
couple days When he was awake, the man called out for his
father but the young man could do nothing aside from tell
him he would be okay without knowing whether it was true
or not."

Joe stopped again. This time it was not because others
came to the bar but because he wanted a refill. Jake took
the order and poured. Then Joe took a sip. Henczel and the
nearest table were not the only ones waiting this time. In fact,
the whole saloon had fallen quiet as they had been listening
and were now waiting. Henczel didn`t ask any questions this
time, he merely waited along with everyone else.

"When the man regained consciousness and was able to
understand the extent of his injuries, he stayed still and talked
to the young man," Joe said, "It turned out that the man was
close to the same age as the young man. They both belonged
to families who had settled farm land. However, the man's
family had been more successful at farming than the young
man's family had been. There were also less people to feed
as many of the family had not survived an illness brought
through by a traveller. The man had gone back east for some
schooling, but had to drop out and go back home because he
had received a letter a month ago that his mother had died
and his father was having issues at the farm.

"The man had been heading back to the family farm when

he had been ambushed by a group of men. He was unsure of how many there had been as it seemed they kept hitting him in the head. They took his horse and all of his belongings, but he felt like they weren't really there to rob him. In an effort to survive, the man had acted like he was dead and after kicking him a few more times they did finally leave him alone.

"As the young man continued to tend to him, the man continued to talk about his life and all the events contained within. The young man listened. But the man didn't get better, no matter what the young man did. It must have been something internal that was broken as nothing external helped. But the man kept talking. It was as if he needed to tell the young man everything before he left this earthly plane. Then one night, the young man woke up to the man's rough breathing. He went over but the man could no longer talk. Instead the young man held the man's hand and provided any comfort he could.

"The young man knew he could not take the man back to his family's farm, so he took what personal items the man had with him and then gave the man a proper burial under the tree. He marked the resting place in the tree trunk before moving on. This time he rode with a destination in mind. The man had given all the information needed to find the farm. It was outside a small town and encompassed a large area to the east of the settlement. The house itself was close to the road on the edge of the property. The young man hesitated a moment but knew he didn't have a choice and knocked on the door.

"The man who answered was not old in appearance but ancient in stature. He looked at the young man with some confusion. The young man stood there and explained how he had come across the man in the ditch. The farmer listened and age seemed to catch up to him with every word spoken. When the young man was finished, the farmer thought for a moment before inviting him for a cup of coffee. The farmer told the young man about his problem, which is why he needed his son back home.

"A businessman from the town wanted to buy the farm, but the farmer didn't want to sell. He was going to be forced to sell if his son didn't come and help out as the farmer was getting too old to work it alone, as well as someone else to help fight against the businessman. The farmer explained the whole situation and the young man listened. Once everything was laid out on the table, both men were quiet for several minutes as they thought the matter over. Finally they talked it out between themselves as the young man explained that his main direction in life was forward and without a specific destination."

Joe paused his story for another sip of his drink. The saloon was quiet as everyone waited for him to continue. A few people took the opportunity to get themselves another drink. Jake poured quickly so the break wouldn't be long. Joe took another sip as he waited for everyone settle back down.

"They came to the same conclusion and agreement. The farmer took the young man on as an adopted son. The young man embraced this as he was familiar with farming as it was what he was raised doing and he had little other skills. With both working the farm, it was much easier and the businessman lost much of his argument for convincing the farmer to sell. It also meant the businessman was faced with two people against his pressure to sell rather than just one. The businessman eventually gave up. The young man settled into his life at the farm. When the farmer died several years later, the young man took over ownership along with the woman he married."

Joe stopped again for another drink. This time a buzz of conversation started as many believed the story finished and they talked about the bits of the story they heard. Henczel was quiet as he waited. A few more people came up for a refill on their drinks. But even when they had gone back to their tables, Joe didn't say anything.

"That can't be the end of it," Henczel said.

"Why not?" Joe asked.

"Because you have not told us who the young man is," Henczel answered.

"Are you expecting me to tell you that?" Joe asked.

"Yes," Henczel answered, "Because otherwise you wouldn't have started the story."

Before Joe could respond, the door to the saloon opened. Sheriff Broddy and Doc McKaig stepped inside. They came around the tables to the bar. Jake offered a drink, but neither accepted.

"Mr. Cheshire has been laid to rest," Sheriff Broddy announced as the room had quieted again. Everyone bowed their heads for a full minute. Afterward, it was quiet as people took sips of their drinks or otherwise seemed to be trying to figure out what to do. Then Mrs. Gilbert stood up.

"He was a great mayor," Mrs. Gilbert said. She sat back down. Mr. Lanaway stood up.

"He was always up for a cup of coffee and long conversation," Mr. Lanaway said before sitting down. Mrs. Jarrett stood up.

"Mr. Cheshire was always such a gentleman," Mrs. Jarrett said and then she sat down.

This started others taking their own turns to say something about the mayor. Mostly it was people at the tables, only when they were finished did Henczel stand up. Joe followed him. Sheriff Broddy said his piece before Doc McKaig said a Bible verse to finish things off. Then everyone bowed their heads again briefly.

While everyone started their own conversations, Henczel turned back to Joe.

"Let's hear the rest of the story," Henczel said.

"The rest of what story?" Broddy asked.

"Joe has been telling us a story," Henczel answered.

"Really?" Broddy asked, "Whose story?"

"We don't know yet," Henczel answered, "We haven't gotten that far. Right now the young man is settling down at the farm he inherited from his adoptive father."

"Well, let's hear the rest of it," Broddy said.

"Do you know who this story is about?" Henczel asked.

"I don't know anything about the story than what you told me," Broddy answered, "But I am willing to hear the end of it, especially if Joe is doing the telling."

The two men turned to Joe and waited for him to start. Those at the nearest tables had also stopped their conversation to listen. The rest continued their conversation as they were not close enough to hear that Joe was continuing the story. Joe took a sip of his drink before he was prepared to start.

"Back when the young man started his journey, he left home with his two possessions," Joe said, "When he inherited the farm, he had only one left. The horse he had stolen back lived for plenty of years and the young man was no longer considered young when the horse passed on from old age. The young man was left with nothing from home, aside from the skills as a farmer he used on a daily basis. He gained something with the work on the farm, one of which was a wife. However, no children came from the relationship."

Joe stopped again for a drink. Broddy opened his mouth to say something but changed his mind when Henczel signalled for him not to speak. More of the people in the saloon had stopped their conversations as they had realized Joe was continuing the story.

"The young man was considered an older man when his wife died," Joe said, "He still had plenty of life left in him, but he was having issues working the farm. He had hired a man to help and felt the man was the best person to leave the farm to when he would have to give it up, though he was sure that was years away.

"The man went into town one day because supplies were needed. While he was there, the man saw several well-dressed men get off the coach. One of them had a pocket watch, which the man recognized even after all the years. The man might have just gone to the sheriff and asked for some help as he had a good relationship with the sheriff, but the man also recognized the man with the pocket watch as one of those who were in the group attacked him so many years earlier.

"The man went back to the farm with the supplies. He dropped things off and then explained to the hired man that he was going back into town. The man also said that if he didn't come back, the hired man had ownership of the farm. The man took with him a horse and his gun, but nothing else. He went to the hotel where the well-dressed men had gone when they had arrived on the stagecoach.

"Most of the well-dressed men were in the dining room, but not the one the man was looking for. However, when he asked at the desk he saw a boy who disappeared as soon as he heard who the man was looking for. The man was directed to a room and headed there. He didn't see the boy again, but the door was open a crack. The man took out his gun and hid it behind his leg before knocking on the door.

"He recognized the voice who invited him in. He opened it slowly to reveal the well-dressed man standing there with a shotgun in his hands pointing at the man. The well-dressed man demanded to know what the man wanted to which the man responded that he wanted his pocket watch back. The well-dressed man denied having stolen the pocket watch and not knowing the man or attacking him. This culminated into an argument between the two. Then the well-dressed man fired the shotgun into the man's leg, which caused the man to collapse to the floor. But before the well-dressed man could fire again, the man shot his own gun and put the bullet through the well-dressed man's head.

"The man took the pocket watch from the well-dressed man's pocket before making his way to out of the hotel dragging his injured leg behind him. The man went to the doctor's office, which is where the sheriff found him. The sheriff listened to the man's story about the attack, being left by the side of the road, and the well-dressed man's denial about the pocket watch. The sheriff gave the man a limited amount of time to get out of town and never return. The sheriff said he should actually arrest the man and charge him with murder, but he understood enough to give the man a chance to leave and start fresh somewhere else."

Joe stopped and took a sip.

"I guess that is the answer to who the story is about," Henczel said.

"Something must have been missed," a man at the nearest table said, "Because I don't understand who."

"It was Mr. Cheshire's life story," Broddy said, "That is where Mr. Cheshire said his limp came from."

"So, the person has to die before you feel you can share their stories," Henczel said to Joe.

"It seemed appropriate for the occasion," Joe shrugged.

"I guess it was," Henczel said. The people in the saloon went back to talking to each other as the story was over and did not hold their attention anymore. Joe finished his drink before having Jake pour him another. Henczel did likewise.

# Chapter Six
## The Horse

Joe came downstairs to find Henczel, Sheriff Broddy and Rachelle sitting at a table while Jake was behind the bar doing inventory. The group at the table had some papers and Henczel was doing most of the talking. Joe sat down in his spot. Jake stopped his inventory long enough to pour Joe a drink. With the drink in front of him, Joe lit himself a cigar.

Jake went into the kitchen for a moment and then came back out to continue his work. Joe took another sip of his drink. Mss. Edwards came out of the kitchen a moment later with a plate of lunch. She set it down in front of Joe before going back to the kitchen. He put his cigar down in the ash tray before starting to eat.

As Joe finished eating, Henczel and Rachelle got up and left the saloon. Sheriff Broddy came over to sit down at the bar next to Joe. He waited as Joe took another sip of his drink.

"What is it?" Joe asked as he reached for his cigar.

"I got a report this morning of a horse spotted running loose outside of ranchlands," Sheriff Broddy answered, "The person believed it was Len's horse, but when they went to talk to Len he wasn't home, so they reported it to me."

"It could be possible that his horse might have gotten loose and run away," Joe said, "But really horses tend to find their way home after a while."

"It means I have to go track down that horse and find out if it's Len's horse," Sheriff Broddy said.

"Let me guess, you are looking for me to go with you," Joe said.

"It would be easier than me explaining to someone else what is happening," Broddy said.

"Well, I did hire Jake because he was competent at his job," Joe said. Jake didn't pause or glance up from his work.

"When did you want to head out?" Joe asked.

"Soon," Broddy answered, "I have to talk to my deputy and get some supplies."

"So, an hour?" Joe asked.

"Sounds about right," Broddy answered. He got to his feet and then left the saloon. Joe finished his drink before getting to his feet.

"When should we expect you back?" Jake asked.

"Eventually," Joe answered, "Since we are going after a horse, it could be a lot longer than I can predict or it could come straight to us without issues. There won't be much point in continuing the search after dark, so I will be back for the night. Is there something I need to know?"

"Two men arrived on the stage this morning and they both have expressed interest in the local poker game," Jake answered.

"If they could be trouble the sheriff wouldn't have let them stay," Joe said, "But if they seem likely to cause trouble get some help from a couple ranchers to keep an eye on them."

Jake nodded. Joe went upstairs. He found his hat and coat. Joe put his coat on and then made sure it was settled correctly. After fixing his hair, Joe put his hat on. Then he went back downstairs. Jake was still working behind the bar. Joe went into the kitchen. Miss. Edwards was busy cleaning up from lunch.

"Do you need something?" Miss. Edwards asked.

"A canteen for water and some dried meat," Joe answered.

"They are over there," Miss. Edwards said pointing toward the pantry.

"Thank you," Joe said. He went to the pantry. Both items were easy to find. Joe took the canteen and filled it with water.

He packed them away before leaving the saloon.

It was easy to tell that it had rained during the night, but it was not raining that moment. But the clouds still hung low enough to suggest it might rain later on.

Joe went to the stables. William was busy with other duties, so Joe got his own horse ready. When he was ready, Joe led his horse out of the stable and mounted outside. He rode to where Broddy was waiting on his horse out front of the saloon. They headed out of town.

"I think you shocked Henczel yesterday," Broddy said, "He thought either you would never tell stories or you were a bad story teller."

"He certainly was surprised when I started into the story," Joe said, "At the beginning he was frustrated with the interruptions, but then he decided no matter what he was going to get me to finish."

"How long did it take for Henczel to figure out who it was about?" Broddy asked.

"The part involving the shotgun," Joe answered, "No one really clued in before that."

"Mr. Cheshire did tell McPherson his whole life story when he put his name forward for the position of mayor," Broddy said, "Didn't they read it back then?"

"I didn't stick to what Mr. Cheshire told McPherson," Joe said, "But the stories were similar enough I thought more people would get it before I got to the end. Henczel got it at the mention of the shotgun and only then."

"He only got it because you gave that part away before now," Broddy said.

"He knew that one before I mentioned it," Joe said, "It was McPherson who didn't know about the shotgun before I gave it away before yesterday. Somehow I thought with all his visits with Mr. Cheshire, Henczel would recognize more of the story."

"I only ever sat with them for coffee on occasion," Broddy

said, "Mr. Cheshire talked about lots of different topics, but not as much on his own history. I think if he hadn't spilled out his whole life story to you while drunk, everyone would think what he told McPherson was the whole story."

"There wasn't much for differences between the stories," Joe said, "Not entirely sure why he felt he needed to tell two versions of it."

"Probably embarrassed about how he had to leave home," Broddy said, "Few people are okay with the fact that they have to leave home due to poverty, especially when their mindset is about being self-sufficient."

"If it wasn't for the shotgun incident, he would have ended up where he started," Joe said, "More successful, but still in stuck on a farm."

"The success is the most important part," Broddy said, "He was a farmer and he didn't really see any reason to move beyond that. He was a good mayor though."

"He was," Joe said, "Now we'll find out how good Henczel is at the job."

"I don't think he will be too bad," Broddy said, "And unless someone else steps up, the town really doesn't have a choice."

"That might mean we have to find another job for Henczel," Joe said, "He can't be the political busy-body forever."

"I keep wondering why he didn't become a lawyer," Broddy said.

"For all the stories he is willing to tell, he hasn't willing to talk about that," Joe said, "Because he did say he started to study law in an attempt to become a lawyer. It was what caused him to not finish he hasn't yet talked about. Maybe someday he will get drunk enough to open up."

"Maybe he is waiting for the day when you both are drunk enough to run your mouths," Broddy said.

"That could be a long time coming," Joe said.

"Likely," Broddy said, "I have watched you drink, I'm not

sure there is enough alcohol in your saloon to get you that drunk. Henczel would take less, but he is careful about how much he drinks and it would take slipping him more than he is used to."

"I don't think making someone drunk against their will is a good way to achieve any goals," Joe said.

"And you haven't done that to achieve one of your goals?" Broddy asked.

"Given that I am one of the people you are talking about getting drunk, it is a method I don't recommend," Joe answered.

"That isn't really an answer," Broddy said.

"Of course, it is," Joe said, "What answer were you expecting?"

"The one you gave me," Broddy said.

"Then why did you ask?" Joe asked.

"Because you have been surprising people lately," Broddy answered, "And sometimes I think if asked at unexpected times you might give me different answers. It hasn't worked so far."

"Perhaps you need to change your methods," Joe said.

"You think it would help?" Broddy asked.

"No," Joe answered, "But it might be entertaining to watch you."

"I'm not sure your entertainment is my priority as far as my actions go," Broddy said.

"Well, if it was you would do things differently," Joe said, "Instead I take my entertainment where I find it."

"Better than those people who create it," Broddy said.

"I've learned to distrust those people," Joe said.

"Then why did you let Scarlett stay?" Broddy asked.

"She hasn't done much for creating any entertainment so far," Joe answered, "Though I fully understand the potential there."

"As long as you aren't keeping her around for your

entertainment," Broddy said.

"No," Joe said, "She can leave whenever she wants to and I'm not going to stand in her way. I would rather she didn't stay to cause problems."

"She starts causing problems and she can get on the next stage," Broddy said.

"Of course," Joe said.

They rode for a while without talking. It started to drizzle. Joe readjusted his hat to avoid getting water in his face. There was little he could do about his clothes getting wet. He would rather be inside his saloon about now, but he couldn't turn back now. Not without a really good reason, of which rain was not one Sheriff Broddy would accept.

"It is only a little bit of rain," Broddy said. Joe could hear the laughter he was trying to keep out of his voice.

"Doesn't mean I have to like it," Joe said.

"Where did you live before that you don't like being outside?" Broddy asked.

"My saloon," Joe answered, "It has this nice thing called a roof, so I don't have to live in the rain and walls to keep the wind out and Miss. Edwards to keep the amount of dirt down."

Broddy shook his head. Joe let the conversation stop there and Broddy didn't try to keep it up.

The rain stayed at the drizzle as they rode. They were getting to the end of the ranches and starting to see unclaimed open space. It wasn't long before they left the ranches behind and it was all open space.

"Now we just need to keep our eyes out for the horse," Broddy said.

"Doesn't Wildman Skinny wander around here?" Joe asked.

"This is known to be his territory," Broddy answered, "But no one has seen him in a couple months and even then he is harmless."

"The stories I have heard suggest he isn't harmless, so

much as he isn't likely to harm anyone without provocation," Joe said.

"I don't see you as likely to try and provoke him," Broddy said.

"I'm not that foolish," Joe said.

"Good," Broddy said.

That was the end of the conversation for a while. The rain stopped giving Joe relief from the falling water. Both men kept their eyes on the horizon in hopes of spotting the horse they were searching for. The clouds kept things from getting too hot.

"You sure his horse was seen out here?" Joe asked after an hour.

"I am sure," Broddy answered, "It can't have gone too far."

Joe sighed and turned his head downward as he shook his head. Then he saw the hoof prints in the sand.

"Well, there was a horse out here at some point," Joe said.

"What do you mean?" Broddy asked.

"Those aren't deep enough for the horse to have a rider, but they are shod," Joe said pointing down. Broddy looked.

"I would say that is what we are looking for," Broddy said.

They changed their direction to follow the hoof prints in the sand. Joe watched them while Broddy watched the horizon for signs of the actual horse. They went along like that for another long while.

The prints went along the sandy for a while and then there was a dip where the hoof prints went down in before going along parallel to the sides of dip. Joe followed them down and then turned with them. Broddy took a step longer to turn before following Joe. They went along this for a while.

"How far can this horse wander?" Joe asked.

"How far can any horse wander," Broddy answered.

"I would assume that it needs to eat at some point," Joe said, "Or find water."

"It should need to do both of those of things," Broddy

said, "And horses usually manage to find their way home too."

"Yet here we are wandering the desert after this horse," Joe said.

"Which is important if this is Len's horse," Broddy said.

"If it is Len's horse," Joe said.

The hoof prints continued forward so the two men did the same. Several minutes later, Joe thought he heard some rumbling. His horse got skittish as did Broddy's horse. Broddy worked to control his horse while looking around.

"Move to higher ground," Broddy shouted.

Joe started to go as ordered, but the rumbling got stronger and the ground was vibrating. His horse stumbled. Joe got down and tried to run while pulling on the reins. He was just about to the edge when the water hit him. The reins were pulled out of his hands and he swept along with the water. It pulled him under. Joe fought his way to the surface to get a breath. A large piece of debris pushed him under again. He tried to work his way up. Just before he felt like his lungs were going to burst, Joe's head broke the surface.

Joe tried to swim with the current and push away any debris that got near him. He was still hit with things. He could not get far enough out of the water to see what happened to his horse or Sheriff Broddy. The muddy water was taking him along the channel it had made during previous flash floods. Joe thought about trying to move towards the edge of that channel, but the push of the water was strong.

Another gasp of air and Joe felt himself pulled under again. He fought his way up. A large piece of debris slammed into him. Joe blacked out.

Joe was aware that he was coughing up muddy water. He was lying on his front in wet sand while there was water falling on his back.

"Dangerous places, those drainage areas," the voice was gruff and not one Joe recognized.

Joe nodded but continued to spit out muddy water and dirt rather than say anything.

"You'd think men such as yourself and the sheriff would know better," the gruff voice continued.

"Sheriff?" Joe managed to croak out.

"Yeah, I got him too," the gruff voice answered, "And your horses."

"Good," Joe said before spitting out more dirt. He did not try to move.

"There is a fire when you are ready," the gruff voice said. Then Joe heard footsteps in the sand of the man walking away.

Joe stayed still several minutes longer. He felt like he had bruises all over his body and was not sure about his ability to move. However, when he did lift his head the muscles worked.

It was still daytime, but the sun was behind black clouds. A short ways away was a camp fire with two people sitting around it and three horses close by. The one person was the sheriff, who looked as badly as Joe felt. The other was a man Joe had never seen before, but who had been described to him. The large amount of unkempt hair with a hat jammed on top and clothing in need another round of patching to add to what was already there. The man himself matched the description of Wildman Skinny.

Using his arms, Joe pulled himself to a sitting position. His clothing was soaking wet and coated with sand. It made him feel grubby and uncomfortable. Joe knew he would feel worse once he was dry. He spit out more dirt that he could feel in his mouth and crunching between his teeth. Joe tried to brush some of the sand off, but it was not helping much.

Joe got up and walked over to the fire. There were pieces of logs to sit on. This looked like Wildman Skinny's regular camping spot, except there was nowhere to sleep visible to Joe. He sat down on one of the logs.

"You all right?" Broddy asked.

"I'm gonna hurt for a few days," Joe answered, "But otherwise I think I will survive. Yourself?"

"Same," Broddy said, "But with added feeling of foolishness. I should have known better."

"You should have," Joe said, "But so should I. We were too focused on our task that we weren't paying attention to the environment we were moving through."

"Foolishness," Wildman Skinny said with a shake of his head.

"Very much so," Broddy said, "And we very much appreciate you pulling us out."

"I may not follow your rules, but others do," Wildman Skinny said, "So, you need to be around to enforce them."

"Maybe you can help us with the reason we are out here and endangering ourselves," Joe said.

"Maybe," Wildman Skinny said, "What brought you out to the desert?"

"Someone said they saw Len Grady's horse out here," Broddy said, "And we were hoping to track it down and get it back."

"Ain't seen Len Grady's horse," Wildman Skinny said, "Only horse out here has been mine. He wanders some, but always finds his way back."

"Well, that is better than chasing a ghost horse," Joe said, "But not much."

"Can't help you," Wildman Skinny said with a shrug.

"You have helped us enough with saving our lives and telling us it was your horse that person saw," Broddy said.

"Probably best if you head back soon," Wildman Skinny said, "So you can reach town before dark falls."

"That is a good idea," Broddy said. He got to his feet. Joe was slower to move as his muscles complained at every movement.

They mounted their horses. Broddy started off in one

direction and Joe followed him. They went until the campfire was no longer visible to them.

"Nice to know my outfit is destroyed chasing a horse owned by a Wildman and nothing to do with your case," Joe said.

"Your clothes can be cleaned," Broddy said.

"Why bother?" Joe asked, "It isn't just the dirt that is the problem, they will not be the same after the other repairs."

"You know many people who wear patched clothes without worry about it," Broddy said.

"That is fine for them," Joe said, "But not for me. I prefer my clothes without repairs."

"It is your clothing and your money," Broddy said.

Joe chose not to respond and instead left Broddy's comment to hang between them. Broddy did not add anything else. The water continued to drum down on them, which did not help Joe's mood. He kept his eyes on the sand and let Broddy guide them towards town.

After a while Joe realized he was seeing hoof prints in the sand heading in the other direction. They were disappearing with the rain hitting the sand and washing them away. Joe could hear Broddy over the rain.

"Ten thousand footprints in the sand; I've travelled far from distant lands."

"The poem you were talking about the other day?" Joe asked.

"Yes," Broddy answered, "There is more."

"Sorry to interrupt," Joe said.

"Ten thousand more have long since faded; like the troubles I long since traded.

Ten thousand nights I've walked alone; in search of what I must atone.

Ten thousand times I've turned around; I held my breath and made no sound.

Ten thousand times I persevered; lost, alone; I disappeared.

Ten thousand promises made and broken; the truth I knew was never spoken.

Ten thousand days I've prayed for solace; a gentle touch; your laugh so flawless.

Ten thousand whispered words of silence; still yet I praise your fierce defiance.

Ten thousand footprints in the sand; you walked beside me; hand in hand."

Joe didn't say anything for several minutes as he finished absorbing the words. Broddy didn't interrupt his thoughts.

"Either I'm better off with philosophy or that wasn't the right poem," Joe said.

"Could be both," Broddy said, "Poetry is subjective. Try Mrs. Gilbert's book of poetry, it might be closer to your tastes."

"I will keep my eye out for it," Joe said.

"There are a few other books that you would probably like," Broddy said, "But I don't have copies to loan you."

"That is okay," Joe said, "I don't think I am quite ready to make the jump from my current reading into poetry."

Broddy shrugged but did not say anything. Once again the two men fell into travelling without speaking. It seemed to Joe that the rain was getting worse, but that may have been his perception. Though it was not as if he could get any wetter.

At that, the sky opened up and a deluge of rain added to what was already coming down. Joe rolled his eyes as his already soaked clothes absorbed more water and weighed him down. His horse did not seem to be enjoying the rain either.

"After forty days of rain,
The man grumbled about pain.
Nothing can be done,
Help came from none
But he hoped the tub would drain."

"What is that?" Broddy asked.

"Something I heard years and years ago," Joe answered, "On another day when it was raining, though I was not as wet at the time."

"It is a limerick," Broddy said, "And it is a type of poetry."

"Well, it is much shorter than the one you recited," Joe said.

"They usually are," Broddy said.

"How do you know so much about poetry?" Joe asked.

"My mother loved all kinds of poetry," Broddy answered, "Her father collected all sorts of books, which she learned to read from a young age. Then she was trained a school teacher, though she never taught in a classroom."

"Why not?" Joe asked.

"During the last month of her training she met my father and once she finished, they married," Broddy answered, "The town where they settled already had a teacher and her training wasn't needed at any point in time. Instead my brothers and I got various types of literature pushed on us as we grew up."

"And it has caused you to read lots of poetry," Joe said.

"Yes," Broddy said, "But I don't mind."

"What happened to your grandfather's books?" Joe asked.

"My uncle inherited them," Broddy answered, "Along with the house."

"That makes sense," Joe said.

"Who taught you to read?" Broddy asked.

"My grandfather," Joe answered, "He felt that being able to read was a very important skill to have."

"It is," Broddy said.

"Depends on what you do with your life," Joe said, "I have met plenty of people who manage to get through life without the ability and others who would be lost without it. As a saloon owner, I find it useful and I enjoy reading in my spare time."

"Mr. Cheshire told me once that as a child he didn't see much point in learning to read," Broddy said, "I was surprised by that at the time."

"He must have decided it was important later," Joe said.

"When he was taken in by the farmer, he decided he should learn to read," Broddy said, "He was never into reading for enjoyment, but he could do his job."

The first post of fencing appeared in the distance through the rain. The hoof prints from earlier were long gone as the rain had washed them from the sand. Until now Joe had depended on Broddy to know they were still heading in the right direction and had not veered off it.

"He preferred to get his information from people," Joe said.

"It probably did him more good as mayor than depending on anything else," Broddy said.

"Very true," Joe said.

They fell silent. The rain slowed a bit but was still soaking Joe. Along with being wet, Joe could feel a chill coming over him as the high from surviving the water was disappearing. His thoughts started to drift from the sandy road ahead to the warm fire crackling in his room. Despite the wet air, Joe could almost smell the faint trace of smoke and burning of a wood fire.

Joe could feel the blanket wrapped around him as well as the heat and light from the fire. There was a cup of tea on the table beside him and it caused a faint scent in the air. Resting his head on the back of the chair and he closed his eyes.

"Hey," Broddy's voice interrupted Joe's thoughts. Joe raised his head and looked around. It was still raining.

"What?" Joe asked.

"Where did you go?" Broddy asked.

"Somewhere warm," Joe answered, "Why did you drag me back?"

"It isn't good to wander like that," Broddy answered, "People don't necessarily come back from those."

"I know," Joe said with a sigh, "But it was nice to be warm, even if it was for a moment. Wise or not."

"Better to be warm when we are back someplace where is it safe," Broddy said.

Joe chose not to say anything in response. This time he did not let his mind wander back to where it was warm. Broddy was right in it being a dangerous place to go. The cold was starting to make Joe's teeth chatter. He held his jaws together in an effort to stop them from knocking against each other.

The two men were getting closer to town as the buildings were closer together. It was hard to see some of them through the rain, but Joe could see enough of them to know how close to town they were. He was almost counting down the places they needed to pass before they reached his saloon.

"Am I losing you again?" Broddy asked.

"Unfortunately, no," Joe answered, "I'm just as wet and miserable as you are."

"I just don't want you to wander so far you don't come back," Broddy said.

"As I said, I'm still here," Joe said, "I just can't wait to get back to warmth and shelter."

"We are almost there," Broddy said.

"I know," Joe said, "But we aren't there yet. And you are the one who dragged me out into the rain to look for a horse that wasn't Len's."

"I thought it might be the horse we needed to find," Broddy said, "You might not have noticed but I am running out leads into Len's murder. I figured finding his horse would help with the case."

"It might still help your case," Joe said, "But somehow I doubt we are going to find the horse out wandering the desert. You are better off looking through people's barns and stables."

"Most people would get upset if I started demanding to look through their property about a murder only a few of us know about," Broddy said, "Otherwise I wouldn't be out wandering the desert in the rain looking for a horse. You may not like being outdoors, but I don't really like wandering in the rain and being half-drowned either. Getting someplace warm sounds good to me too."

"The next time you want to wander the desert you can tell someone else about the murder and they can get caught in the rain," Joe said.

"I will take that into consideration," Broddy said.

Joe just watched more water drip off his hat and onto the saddle. His coat felt heavier with more added to it. Joe could feel the pain in his jaw from trying to stop his teeth from chattering. The pull of warmth was there, but this time he felt like he would not actually come back if he visited it.

Through the rain more buildings became visible and Joe realized they had reached town. The idea of being close to his saloon and thus his home filled Joe was relief. Even his horse seemed happier to be in town and close to the stable.

As they got the close to the stable, Broddy went off towards his office. Joe went to the stables. He left his horse with William and slogged his way to the back door of the saloon. Miss. Edwards barely looked up at Joe as he made his way through, but she did start to put the kettle on. Joe went into the main room. No one noticed as he slipped through and up the stairs.

Once inside his suite, Joe stripped off his soaking wet clothes and dropped them into the basket with the rest of his laundry. He dried himself off before putting on clean clothing. Joe made sure the fireplace was ready before he dropped a lit match on to the wood. Just as he was pulling out a blanket, there was a knock at the door. Joe opened it and Miss. Edwards was standing there with a tray. On the tray were a tea pot, a cup, and a plate of supper.

"Thank you," Joe said as he accepted the tray.

"You are welcome," Miss. Edwards said.

She headed back down the hall while he took the tray inside his room and closed the door. He set the tray on the table by the chair. Joe wrapped himself up in the blanket before sitting down and settling in for the evening.

# Chapter Seven
## Suspicious Behaviour

Joe felt much more himself when he came downstairs the next day. He returned the tray to the kitchen, where Miss. Edwards was making lunch, before sitting in his spot at the end of the bar. Joe lit himself a cigar but skipped the drink. Jake was behind the bar checking inventory and cleaning.

A moment later Miss. Edwards came out of the kitchen with a plate of lunch for Joe. He set the cigar in the ashtray and started to eat. Once he was finished, Joe returned the plate to the kitchen. When he came back out to the main room, Henczel was sitting at the bar. Jake was still doing his work and had not stopped to pour Henczel a drink. Joe came back to his seat and picked up his cigar again.

"What kind of trouble is going on in town?" Joe asked as he exhaled a cloud of smoke.

"I wouldn't call it trouble per say," Henczel answered.

"You are here in the middle of the day," Joe said.

"Two gentlemen arrived yesterday," Henczel said, "They had expressed interest in gambling when they got off the stage."

"Jake said something about them yesterday," Joe said, "But I left with the sheriff before I could meet them."

"I wondered where you two went," Henczel said, "But that is beside the point. The one gentleman did play once DeWhite had the game going, but the other spent time talking to people."

"What is the gentleman looking for?" Joe asked.

"A man," Henczel answered, "I didn't speak with him

directly, but based on what I overheard he is looking for Mr. Cheshire; though he didn't say that outright."

"He may not know him by the name Mr. Cheshire," Joe said, "So, he may not know to ask for him by that name."

"I believe Mr. Cheshire was his name," Henczel said, "Making it unlikely for someone to know him as something else."

"Why do you think a man looking for Mr. Cheshire is trouble?" Joe asked, "And have you talked to the sheriff about the matter yet?"

"Broddy let them stay yesterday after he questioned them when they arrived on the stage," Henczel answered, "I think these men might be more trouble than he does."

"Did you happen to overhear why he was looking for Mr. Cheshire?" Joe asked.

"He didn't say anything straight out," Henczel answered, "But the impression I got was that the man was a relative."

"You spent as much time with him as anyone, do you remember Mr. Cheshire mentioning any relatives?" Joe asked.

"Not in any current context," Henczel said, "It sounded more like he left them behind when he left the family farm and hadn't heard from any of them since then. That is part of why I am suspicious of these men."

"Not sure there is much we can do," Joe said, "These men haven't done anything yet and the sheriff has determined they can stay for now. Until we can show they are up to no good, we are going to have to wait to see what they are going to do."

"I suppose," Henczel said, "But I still think they are suspicious."

"I'm not saying they aren't," Joe said, "Perhaps you should discuss the matter with the sheriff again and this time tell him about what you overheard."

"No one has seen him yet today," Henczel said, "The deputy said no one has seen the sheriff since he left with you yesterday."

"Someone thought they saw a runaway horse in the desert," Joe said, "And it rained on us while we were out looking for it. He likely went home to warm up and is just sleeping in."

"Then I will try looking for him again," Henczel said getting up, "He doesn't usually sleep in this late."

Henczel left the saloon. Joe did not move for several minutes.

"Why am I suddenly the person to bring the world's problems to?" Joe asked out loud.

"Because you have spent the last while getting into business that isn't yours," Jake answered.

Joe nodded almost to himself.

"Anything else happen last night?" Joe asked.

"No," Jake answered.

"Good," Joe said. He stubbed out the end of his cigar before getting up to help Jake.


Broddy was still tired and half-asleep as he sat at his kitchen table. His hands were wrapped around the cup of coffee trying to get as much of the heat from the cup as possible. He knew he should already be in his office, but between sleeping in and being in pain he was not in a rush to go anywhere.

There was a knock at the front door. Broddy pulled his fingers from around the cup and tugged the blanket tighter around his shoulders before he stood up. He went to the door and opened it. Henczel was standing outside.

"Yes?" Broddy asked.

"I wanted to talk to you about the men who arrived on the stage yesterday," Henczel answered, "Are you okay?"

"I will be," Broddy answered. After a moment of thought, Broddy held the door for Henczel to enter. Then Broddy closed the door before returning to his chair. Henczel settled into the chair across from Broddy.

"What about the men?" Broddy asked. He remembered

Henczel coming to him yesterday about the same men. The one man had been a gambler and the other had claimed to be a railroad clerk taking some time off.

"The one man spent yesterday asking around about someone," Henczel answered, "I think he was looking for Mr. Cheshire. It doesn't feel right to me."

"I can't tell someone to move along because you don't like them," Broddy said, "And if he really wants to find Mr. Cheshire, he is a little late. If you find him trying to dig Mr. Cheshire up, I will put him in the cell until the next stage comes through."

"I just feel like letting them stay is going to be a problem," Henczel said.

"Have they broken any laws yet?" Broddy asked.

"No," Henczel answered.

"Then there is nothing I can do about them," Broddy said, "And nothing I will do unless they do cause trouble. If the man is looking for Mr. Cheshire, maybe the best thing to do is to just tell him what happened and then let him move along on his own."

Henczel was quiet and Broddy could feel the frustration coming off him. Maybe if Broddy was not as tired and sore he might be taking Henczel more seriously. He remembered feeling suspicious about the man, but not enough to ask him to leave town. Since Henczel was also suspicious of the man, he would keep an eye on the man.

"Should he do anything illegal, I will deal with him," Broddy said.

"Fine," Henczel said but his tone suggested otherwise. He got up and went to the door. Opening the door, he found Miss. Modahl standing there getting ready to knock.

"I'm sorry," Miss. Modahl said as she lowered her hand.

"It is okay," Henczel said, "I was just leaving."

Miss. Modahl stepped out of the way and let Henczel go before she entered the house. She closed the door before turning to Broddy.

"Are you okay?" Miss. Modahl asked as she came to the table.

"Just stayed out in the rain too long yesterday," Broddy answered.

"Your deputy is worried," Miss. Modahl said, "Because he hadn't heard from you this late in the day."

"I'll go in to relieve him as soon as I warm up," Broddy said.

"You go back to bed," Miss. Modahl said, "And I will make you soup."

Broddy thought about arguing with her, but she was already getting ready to start the soup. He took another mouthful of the lukewarm coffee before getting up and taking his blanket back to bed.

Joe was back in his spot, this time with a drink, when Henczel came back in. The saloon was half-full and the card game was already going. Henczel sat down near Joe and ordered a drink.

"I found the sheriff," Henczel said.

"Glad he hadn't disappeared," Joe said.

"He is visiting Miss. Modahl," Henczel said.

"Not really a surprise," Joe said, "I am guessing that he did not agree to run the gentlemen out of town."

"He refuses to do anything about them unless they actually do something against the law," Henczel said.

"That is his job," Joe said.

"I suppose it is," Henczel said. Henczel focused on his drink.

"You are more morose than usual," Joe said.

"I'm just worried," Henczel said.

"Why don't you just ask the man what he is looking for?" Joe asked.

"I doubt he would tell me the truth," Henczel answered, "Last night it sounded a lot more like he was trying not to give up too much information. His behaviour is off for someone who is looking for a relative. I learned long ago that when something felt off there was usually a good reason why."

"I may be a member of town council, but I am only a lowly saloon owner," Joe said, "Nothing I can do about suspicious people and their motives."

"Mr. Cheshire considered you a friend," Henczel said.

"That was nice of him," Joe said, "But doesn't change what I can do."

Henczel nodded as once again focused on his drink. This time Joe did not interrupt his thoughts. Joe's eyes strayed over the rest of the room. All the usual regulars were there, but the gentlemen Henczel had talked about were not. Likely more people would come later as they finished up with supper and came for a drink before heading for bed. DeWhite was seated at his usual spot with Miss. Karina on one side and Shorty Jennings on the other. They were all focused on the game. There was still another seat available, but no one appeared ready to fill it. Someone would later, Joe was sure.

Movement out of the corner of his eye caused Joe to turn his head a little bit. Scarlett had come down the stairs. She was wearing a dress that matched her name and showed a bit more than was appropriate for a lady. Her hair was carefully put up. She looked like she was ready for the evening. Scarlett sat down at a table, but her closed position did not suggest she wanted company. Joe turned back to Henczel, who was still absorbed with his drink.

The door of the saloon opened and two gentlemen stepped inside. They were both dressed in suits, one grey and the other brown. The man in the brown suit went straight to the game. He asked about the empty seat and was invited to join. The man in the grey suit started wandering towards the bar. He greeted some people he had met before on his way.

"This the problem?" Joe asked in a quiet voice.

Henczel glanced over his shoulder and then focused again on his drink.

"Yup," Henczel answered.

The man arrived at the bar and ordered a drink. Jake poured it in exchange for coinage. The man sat down beside Henczel.

"Someone said you were running for mayor," the man said to Henczel.

"Is there a question you want to ask or just spread gossip?" Henczel asked.

"I'm just trying to make conversation," the man answered.

"What makes you think I want to talk to you?" Henczel asked.

"It was suggested that I talk to you," the man answered, "So, that is what I am trying to do."

"And who are you that someone suggested you talk to me?" Henczel asked.

"The owner of the hotel," the man answered, "He said you know Samuel Cheshire."

"What's it to you?" Henczel asked.

"I am looking for him," the man answered, "And no one seems to know where I can find him."

"Why would you be looking for him?" Henczel asked.

"He is my father," the man answered.

"And your name is?" Henczel asked.

"Justin Cheshire," the man answered.

Henczel glanced at Joe over his drink without raising his head. Joe did not change his facial expression as he met Henczel's eyes.

"I don't recall Mr. Cheshire mentioning you in all the conversations I have had with him," Henczel said.

"Given his history, I am not surprised he didn't tell you everything," Justin said, "He was not necessarily always on the right side of the law."

"Mr. Cheshire admitted to not always being on the right

side of the law," Henczel said, "He even mentioned Steven, but he never talked about you."

"Unfortunately that is what happens when parents have a favourite child," Justin said.

Joe moved his head to survey the room rather than meet Henczel's eyes again. More people had come in and the room was filling up. Joe felt his eyes drawn to the table where Scarlett was sitting. She had gotten a drink, but otherwise was still sitting alone. He did not turn his head further to see more and instead kept his eyes moving across the crowd. She was pretending to ignore him.

"I will take your word on that," Henczel said, "As my parents didn't have a favourite and I have no children. Aside from him being your father, why are you looking for Mr. Cheshire?"

"That is not a good enough reason?" Justin asked.

"Well, he has never mentioned you and you just admitted to not being his favourite child," Henczel answered, "It seems strange to me that you would come looking for him."

"I need to talk to him about family," Justin said, "We may not have been close, but family is important to him."

"That was true," Henczel said with a nod.

Joe looked up sharply at Henczel and was met with a mischievous spark in Henczel's eyes. Using a sip from his drink, Joe hid the shake of his head. His eyes were drawn back across the room to where Scarlett was sitting at the table with her own drink. Joe let his eyes go over everyone else in the saloon before coming back to Henczel and Justin. So far there was no trouble among those who had come to drink and play cards.

"So, you know how important it is for me to find my father," Justin said.

"I'm starting to," Henczel said.

The door to the saloon opened and McPherson entered. He came over to the bar and took the seat next to Joe.

"Good evening," McPherson said once he had asked Jake for a drink.

"Evening," Joe said.

"Quiet evening?" McPherson asked.

"Matt and Michael are going to be putting on a show within the next few drinks unless something more exciting happens," Joe answered, "Nothing exciting for you this evening?"

"No," McPherson answered.

"The gentleman on the other side of you is Justin Cheshire," Joe said. McPherson glanced at Joe was a raised eyebrow before looking over.

"Really?" McPherson asked.

"I am," Justin answered.

"I am Kevin McPherson," McPherson said, "I am the newspaper editor here in town. Are you related to Samuel Cheshire?"

"He is my father," Justin answered.

"Really?" McPherson asked. He dug into his pocket and pulled out a notebook along with the sub of a pencil. He licked the tip of the pencil before putting it to the page to make a note. "What are you doing in town?"

"I am looking for my father," Justin said.

McPherson nodded as he wrote more down.

"It must have been a while since you have seen him," McPherson said.

Joe glanced at Henczel, but Henczel appeared to be paying attention to the interaction between McPherson and Justin. McPherson was as suspicious of Justin as Henczel but was going about things slightly differently. They were going to figure out what was really going on. Joe's eyes scanned the room. It was the same as the last time he checked on it. His eyes went to Scarlett. She was still sitting there with her drink pretending to ignore him.

"Far too many years," Justin said, "I have spent the last six months trying to track him down. It has been a difficult trip as he left very little trace."

"I imagine it must be really hard," McPherson said, "It must be a really important matter for you to spend so much time and energy to find him again."

"Family is very important," Justin said, "And also the matter I need to talk to him about."

Rancher Anders entered the saloon. Joe watched him find a table to sit. It was off to one side of the room and one of the few left empty. Joe wondered what brought Anders in because he did not usually come into town to drink. He hoped there would not be trouble there. Joe scanned the rest of the room. DeWhite did not seem happy with the man in the brown suit, but he was not yet to the point of throwing him out of the game. Michael and Matt were settling down rather than getting louder. They might still cause a scene but not yet.

Joe tried not to let his eyes drift to Scarlett. They did anyway. She pretended she did not notice, but she was as aware of him as he was of her. He did not want to be. Joe would have rather concentrated on his business, or even what Henczel and McPherson were doing to Justin. He had lost the thread of the conversation they were having right next to him.

"Unfortunately, it is the rainy season," Henczel said, "Making it not a good idea to wander too far into the desert. Otherwise it might be able to happen."

"That really is unfortunate," Justin said, "Are you sure there isn't another way?"

"We are sure," McPherson answered, "Just ask Joe."

Justin looked to Joe for an answer.

"Of course," Joe said, "They don't have any reason to lie to you."

McPherson gave Joe a nod for giving the right answer. Joe took a sip of his drink in an effort to maintain his expression. He found it to be the last sip in the glass. Joe moved the glass for Jake to refill it. When it was full, he moved it back and took a sip; which ended up being more than a sip as half the glass disappeared down his throat. He put the glass down before he drank the rest too fast.

"I suppose him being a recluse makes sense," Justin said, "He did make it difficult to find him. How long do you think it will be before it is safe to travel to the caves?"

"It has been pretty bad the last few days, so likely within the next two days," McPherson answered, "We can usually tell when the bad period is almost over as the rains gets worse and then better from there. If it rains tonight then things are almost over."

"And if it doesn't rain tonight?" Justin asked.

"Then we haven't seen the worst of the storms," Henczel answered.

"Are you sure it isn't possible to go out to the cave earlier?" Justin asked.

"Not a good idea," Joe answered, "I wasn't paying enough attention to the weather when I went out there the other day to talk to him."

"What happened?" Justin asked.

"I just about drowned," Joe answered.

"In the desert?" Justin asked.

"Happens all the time," Henczel answered, "We get reports and bodies showing up all the time. The water gathers and then you get a whole river where there was nothing but a slight impression seconds earlier. It can take out men and horses and even larger animals."

"And when this happens who checks on my father?" Justin asked.

"We all take turns except when the rains show up," Henczel answered, "Then we wait until the rains are over before going back out. He is usually okay during those times."

"How was he when you visited him?" Justin asked Joe.

"A little quiet," Joe answered.

McPherson gave Joe a warning look but Justin just nodded.

Joe absently picked up his glass and took a sip. His eyes wandered over the patrons of the saloon. He noticed that Anders had a bottle and a glass now in front of him. There were a couple of glasses missing from the bottle; not enough for him to be drunk and since he was still staring at the liquid in the glass with a hard focus the alcohol was not working yet.

Joe tried not to spend much time looking at the side of the room where Scarlett was sitting but he could not stop himself from lingering a second too long. She was still sitting there with her drink. One of the girls who rented a room upstairs was sitting with her. The girl was flashing her smile at any man who appeared to have money for her time but the men were still sober enough to not be ready for that service. She would get more business later.

Joe tried to take another sip of his drink and found the glass to be empty. He moved it over to have Jake refill it. Jake finished serving someone else before coming back to pour Joe's drink. Some part of Joe's brain was sending him a warning about how much he was drinking tonight but he just took another sip of alcohol to quiet it down. After his sip, Joe put his glass down.

"But you think it should be possible to go out there within the week?" Justin asked.

"Should be," McPherson answered, "As much as it must be frustrating to be so close and not be able to go farther at the moment."

"It has taken this long to find him," Justin said, "A few more days shouldn't matter too much, I suppose."

"I know this small town isn't very interesting," Henczel said, "But we will take you out to see Mr. Cheshire as soon as we can."

"I appreciate that," Justin said.

Joe's eyes were drawn to the poker game where DeWhite was frowning at Justin's companion. It still was not enough for DeWhite to kick him out of the game, but he definitely was not happy with the man. On another night Joe might have wandered over to see what the problem was but tonight he was choosing not to move from his place. If DeWhite wanted to kick the man out, that was up to DeWhite. Miss. Karina was trying to keep smiling from her position next to DeWhite, but anyone who knew her could see it was not real. That may have been part of the issue between DeWhite and the man.

Henczel and Justin moved to a table for further discussion about something. McPherson made no move to join the. He finished his drink but shook his head at Jake's offer to refill his glass. Then he turned to Joe.

"You weren't really out in that storm yesterday, were you?" McPherson asked.

"Unfortunately I was," Joe answered.

"Why?" McPherson asked.

"Sheriff Broddy asked for help tracking down a runaway horse," Joe answered.

"And he asked you for help?" McPherson asked.

"Yes," Joe answered.

"I would have thought he would pick someone more inclined to work with horses over you who prefers not to get his boots dirty," McPherson said.

"He had some excuse when he came to me asking for me to help him," Joe said, "I just can't remember what it was now."

"Must have been a good one," McPherson said.

"So, what are you going to do to him?" Joe asked.

"Probably abandon him in a rocky area," McPherson answered, "We will need to talk about it before we head out."

"I may have missed a few points in the conversation," Joe said, "But have you two figured out why Justin is looking for Mr. Cheshire? And are you taking his friend with him to the caves? Because DeWhite might be happy for the man to disappear."

McPherson glanced over his shoulder at the game. Once he had assessed the situation he turned back.

"We aren't leaving soon enough," McPherson said, "DeWhite is going to have to deal with that issue himself."

"As long as it doesn't mean blood on my floor," Joe said.

"I think he knows that," McPherson said, "Though it is an easy thing to forget when in the middle of an upsetting situation."

Out of the corner of his eye, Joe saw the girl with Scarlett get up and head upstairs with a man. Scarlett stayed with her drink.

"I almost thought Matt and Michael were going to fix more furniture tomorrow," McPherson said, "But they seem to have settled down."

"For now," Joe said, "They may still get there. Depends on if they feel people need more entertainment for the evening."

"There is enough potential here without them," McPherson said.

"I believe that is why they have settled down," Joe said.

McPherson nodded. They did not speak for several minutes. Joe took another sip of his drink. He looked over the room. The situation at the game had not changed. Anders was much farther into the bottle and was starting to focus on other things than his drink. Joe's eyes found Scarlett glancing his direction but she quickly looked somewhere else when she realized he was looking her way. Joe pretended he did not notice.

"Based on what we have gotten from him, I don't believe he has any good intentions towards Mr. Cheshire," McPherson said, "If he did, he would be much more willing to tell us what he wanted with our mayor. Instead he lied to us about being Mr. Cheshire's son. Unless there is a son no one knows about and he wasn't willing to admit to."

"Considering what else he did tell us about, I doubt he had a son he didn't tell us about," Joe said, "But he did leave men behind who were upset with him."

"One would hope that Justin and his friend are not here to kill Mr. Cheshire," McPherson said.

"Maybe it is me," Joe said, "but does it matter at this point?"

"Well, not to Mr. Cheshire," McPherson said, "But to the rest of us, yes."

"I suppose there are worse things to do with your time," Joe said, "And as long as neither man offers to kill you or Henczel for your fun."

"I think we will be okay," McPherson said.

DeWhite's voice could be heard over the other conversations, but the exact words were lost between him and Joe. Quiet settled over the room as everyone's attention was directed toward DeWhite and the man. Both had gotten to their feet. DeWhite's hand was heading toward his knife. The man also appeared to be reaching for a hidden weapon. They stood and faced each other as everyone else in the saloon waited to see what was going to happen next.

"Going to remind him about not wanting blood on your floor?" McPherson asked in a whisper.

"No," Joe answered quietly. He took another sip of his drink.

"That is it?" McPherson asked in the same volume.

Joe shrugged and continued to drink.

"I told you to back off," DeWhite said, "Get out,"

"Why should I?" the man asked.

"This is my game," DeWhite answered, "My rules. Get out or there is going to be trouble."

"Going to be trouble?" there was a sneer in the man's voice.

"Get out," DeWhite voice went hard. Something must have passed between the two men as they stood there challenging each other. The man's hand stopped and he backed down.

"Fine," the man said. He took his money off the table and stepped away from the game. He left the saloon. There was a pause before DeWhite sat back down. The game restarted.

Slowly the rest of the room went back to their conversations and drinking. Joe glanced at the table where Henczel and Justin were talking. Justin made no move to follow his friend out.

"So, there was some entertainment for the evening," McPherson said, "Now Matt and Michael don't need to start breaking furniture with each other."

"Doesn't mean they won't," Joe said, "Just that they aren't likely to."

"You really depended on DeWhite to remember you don't want a fight in here," McPherson said.

"I didn't feel like getting up," Joe said. He finished his drink and set the glass down on the bar. Jake refilled it without being asked.

"That is it?" McPherson asked.

Joe shrugged rather than saying anything.

"You aren't drunk," McPherson said.

"Probably just tired," Joe said, "Yesterday was a long day. Why are you so worried?"

"Henczel and I might need your help with the situation," McPherson answered, "And that means I don't want to turn to you to have you unavailable."

"I should be around," Joe said, "But don't expect me for much."

"That is what I do expect," McPherson said.

Justin got up from the table and then wandered toward the door. He was trying to appear like he was just done for the night, rather than following his friend. He left the saloon and the door swung closed behind him. Henczel got up from the table and went back to the bar to sit down.

"Anything else?" McPherson asked as Henczel nodded to Jake for a refill.

"Not that is applicable to our plan," Henczel answered.

"Anything interesting anyway?" McPherson asked. Henczel took a sip of his drink before answering.

"He and his friend haven't been travelling together long," Henczel answered, "They started because they were going in the same direction and there were rumours about danger to travellers."

"Doesn't sound much like hired killers," McPherson said.

"Justin might be," Henczel said, "But his friend isn't."

"They might be here to get the watch back," Joe said.

"Rachelle owns it now," Henczel said, "And there is no reason to get it from her. Though if they are only here for the watch, it would be hard to explain to Mr. Cheshire why Justin is lying about being his son. Why not make up a better story? Be a friend of the family or have something to give to Mr. Cheshire with some made up reason?"

"Maybe he is just a bad liar," Joe said, "And the only reason he is even talking to anyone is that he can't find Mr. Cheshire by himself. What is his friend's problem?"

"He didn't really explain his friend's behaviour," Henczel answered, "You would have to ask DeWhite what the issue was."

"I'm in no rush," Joe said, "But if it is a lingering issue, you might not want to wait too long before your cave adventure."

"We need to figure out where exactly we are taking them," McPherson said.

"There are some great areas to the south," Henczel said.

"If we pick the right area out there, they may never come out," McPherson said.

"As long as they don't come back here and report to the sheriff that you two tried to kill them," Joe said.

"They apparently don't know much about wandering the desert," Henczel said, "If they find their way back here, we can say they wandered away and we couldn't find them."

"I hope you find something more believable than that," Joe said, "You are planning murder and Sheriff Broddy knows you both well enough to know when you are lying."

"But we reported the two men missing when we come back

to town without them," Henczel said, "Doesn't that prove we didn't want to kill them?"

"Depends partly on whether Sheriff Broddy hears about your plan," Joe said.

"Are you going to start telling stories?" Henczel asked.

Joe did not answer. Instead he moved his empty glass over for Jake to refill it. It took a moment because he had to wander back after pouring a drink for someone else. Once the glass was refilled, Joe took a sip.

"You seem to be drinking more tonight," Henczel said.

"McPherson already bothered me on that point," Joe said, "And I explained that yesterday was a long day out in the desert, which means I am tired today."

"It rained yesterday," Henczel said.

"You are very perceptive," Joe said.

"Why would you ever be out in the rain in the desert?" Henczel asked, "You barely leave your saloon when it is pleasant outside."

"I got asked to help Sheriff Broddy go after a runaway horse," Joe said, "Because I am on the town council and he wanted an official presence for the activity."

"Strange," Henczel said, "Did he give you a longer explanation?"

"Like what?" Joe asked.

"It usually has to be a very serious matter before a member of the town council accompanies the sheriff on a matter," Henczel answered, "A runaway horse doesn't sound important enough for that. What else was involved?"

"If it is a matter for a town council member, why would I start telling you?" Joe asked, "Why don't you ask Sheriff Broddy?"

"Because we are sitting here talking to you," Henczel answered.

"That sounds a lot like telling stories," Joe said.

"You do know that telling stories in a normal thing for

people to do, right?" McPherson asked, "If people didn't tell stories, I wouldn't have a job. Even more people like reading and hearing stories. It isn't wrong to tell stories."

"Doesn't mean I need to start telling them," Joe said.

"I liked listening to you telling us about Mr. Cheshire's life," McPherson said.

"He wasn't around to complain about me telling it," Joe said, "But other people might complain about me telling other stories. In this instance, Sheriff Broddy."

"Did he ask you not to?" Henczel asked, "Because if he didn't, you can tell us."

"Doesn't matter," Joe answered.

"Well, we can't ask him tonight," Henczel said, "He is visiting Miss. Modahl this evening."

"I keep wondering if he will propose to her," McPherson said.

"Not yet," Joe said.

"Why not?" McPherson asked.

"Because he feels he needs a proper house before he gets himself a wife," Joe answered.

"Really?" McPherson asked.

"You have never asked him?" Henczel asked, "He tells that to everyone who asks him about marrying Miss. Modahl."

"No, I have never asked him," McPherson answered, "I keep expecting him to tell me to put the engagement announcement in the paper."

"Only at Miss. Modahl's insistence," Henczel said, "Because I am not sure he would tell you on purpose without that."

"Don't you have a fiancée you left in the east until you made your fortune?" Joe asked McPherson.

"Every newspaper job in the east requires experience or a rich family," McPherson answered, "So, I came out west hoping to get the experience required for a job at a newspaper. I wasn't really expecting to run a newspaper. The other option has been to find a way to make a fortune in an effort to fill the other way to get the job."

"How does she feel on the matter?" Joe asked.

"She has been okay with it," McPherson answered, "We write to each other weekly and she promised to wait. I have stayed true to her despite the distance. Did you ever marry?"

"I was engaged once," Henczel answered, "Back when I was in school. She was the prettiest girl I had laid eyes on. Her sweetness drew me further in love with her. I begged her to marry me before anyone else could court her."

"So, what happened?" McPherson asked.

"Her parents were willing to let the engagement stand as long as I was working towards being a lawyer," Henczel answered, "Being married to a lawyer was okay for their daughter as then she would be taken care of properly."

"But you aren't a lawyer," McPherson said.

"Hence why I am not married," Henczel said.

"You didn't ask her to run away with you when you came west?" McPherson asked.

"It hardly seemed appropriate to ask such a thing of her," Henczel answered.

"You must have really loved her," Joe said.

"I did," Henczel said nodding his head.

"Why would not running away with her mean he loved her?" McPherson asked.

"Because he wanted her to find happiness with someone who would take proper care of her, rather than taking her where it would be a rougher life," Joe said.

"How do you know that?" McPherson asked Joe.

"Get away from me!" Scarlett's voice caught Joe's attention. Somehow he had gotten distracted from his obsession with her and quit looking over to her. He looked and saw Anders was trying to grab Scarlett to take her upstairs. His actions suggest he was drunk, but he was still stronger than she was. Scarlett was working to avoid his hands. The rest of the people in the saloon quieted down as they turned to watch.

Anders managed to catch Scarlett's arm. She hit him in an effort to get him let go, but he was not bothered by it.

Joe barely realized he was moving until he had his fist hitting Ander's face. This caused Anders to let go of Scarlett. She hurried away to avoid being in the middle of a fight. Anders stumbled backward and on to his backside. Joe grabbed Anders's coat and pulled him to his feet. Joe took him between the tables and right out the swinging half-doors. There was enough speed gathered on the way out that when Joe let Anders, he went flying into the middle of the road.

"Never bother my guest again," Joe said.

Anders groaned but did not immediately move. Joe went back inside. He went back to his seat at the bar. Everyone was quiet for a short period before they went back to their conversations. Scarlett had been standing there. She came over to the bar.

"Thank you," Scarlett said quietly. Then she headed up the stairs. Joe finished his drink and then set it for Jake to refill it.

# Chapter Eight
## The Shiny Button

Joe had not been up long when Sheriff Broddy entered the saloon. Jake and Miss. Edwards were off somewhere else. No one else had shown up, despite Joe half-expecting to wake up to Henczel and McPherson already there. Sheriff Broddy sat down near Joe.

"A drink?" Joe asked holding up his own glass.

"I'm working," Sheriff Broddy answered.

"I'm not going anywhere today," Joe said.

"I'm not here to ask you to go anywhere," Sheriff Broddy said, "Apparently there was some fun last night in here."

"Two men came to town recently and they were in here last night," Joe said, "The one spent the time talking to McPherson and Henczel while the other joined the game. At some point in the evening, DeWhite kicked the man out of the game. I didn't go over and ask why. The man left without further issue. You were better off asking DeWhite about the matter."

"I already talked to him," Sheriff Broddy said, "He kicked the man out of the game due to the man leering at and making rude comments towards Miss. Karina."

"Makes sense to why he would object to the man being there," Joe said.

"That wasn't the incident I wanted to speak with you about," Sheriff Broddy said, "I have heard from plenty of people who say you kicked someone out last night as well."

"Anders came in to drink," Joe said, "He got drunk and mistook the guest for one of the working girls. When she refused his advances, he got violent and I sent him out the door. I'm pretty sure he walked away as he was not injured when he left."

"You didn't throw him out for other reasons?" Sheriff Broddy asked.

"I didn't," Joe answered, "I would have left him alone if he hadn't made a scene, but he chose to do so."

"Okay," Sheriff Broddy said.

"No crimes were committed in here last night," Joe said.

"From the sounds of it, there wasn't," Sheriff Broddy said, "But I have to make sure."

"Anders didn't report it to you," Joe said.

"He didn't," Sheriff Broddy said, "I doubt he would whether you had injured him or not."

"So, anything else you need to know?" Joe asked.

"I would like to know what Henczel and McPherson are up to," Sheriff Broddy answered, "They have had their heads together all morning and refuse to say anything on the matter."

"Why should I know what they are doing?" Joe asked.

"Because they are more likely to talk to you about such things than anyone else," Sheriff Broddy answered, "Which makes you an accomplice."

"I don't think that would hold up in court," Joe said.

"A pity," Sheriff Broddy said, "If that were the case, I might get you to actually tell me what is going on."

Sheriff Broddy got to his feet.

"I'll let you get back to work," Sheriff Broddy said.

"Good day to you too," Joe said.

Sheriff Broddy left the saloon.

DeWhite was one of the first people to come in. He sat down at the table to set up the game. Joe was behind the bar. He had already poured himself a drink and was sipping it as he waited for people to come in. Joe did not really pay attention to DeWhite. Once the table was set up, DeWhite came over to the bar and ordered a drink.

"Is that man expected again?" DeWhite asked as Joe poured the drink.

"I would hope no," Joe answered, "But I didn't ban him or his friend."

DeWhite nodded before taking his drink back to the table. Shorty entered the saloon and took up his usual position. Joe knew that Miss. Karina would come down when some of the other girls did. A few men came in. Joe poured drinks as they were ordered. The men settled in.

The saloon slowly filled up. Joe tended to his customers. Aside from Matt and Michael glaring at each other occasionally, there was no trouble. Justin and his friend had not tried to come in; neither did Henczel and McPherson. Joe wondered if it was going to be a quiet evening. They did happen sometimes. Matt and Michael could start fighting if nothing else happens, but Joe was not worried about them as they would fix anything they broke.

Scarlett had not come down for the evening. She had been down briefly for supper. However, she did not appear to want to stay for a drink. Joe understood. They had not talked about what happened or their relationship. He did not expect them to any time soon, though they probably spend more time together before she decided to move along. Because she would move along.

The saloon door swung open. Joe barely glanced up from the drink he was pouring to see Sheriff Broddy enter. The man took his drink and went back to the table. Sheriff Broddy sat down where the man had been.

"Expecting trouble?" Joe asked.

"No," Sheriff Broddy answered, "But after hearing everything from last night, I figured it might be best if I spend some time here."

"Drink?" Joe asked.

"Sure," Broddy answered.

Joe poured the drink and set it in front of Broddy, who took a sip before putting the drink down. He was quiet as he looked over the crowd. Sheriff Broddy studied anyone who might seem slightly like they could be trouble. His eyes stayed on Matt and Michael longer than anyone else. Finding no current possibility of trouble, Broddy took another sip of his drink.

"Did you figure it out?" Joe asked.

"Not yet," Broddy answered, "But it has something to do with the two men who arrived the other day. One of the two men is looking for Mr. Cheshire, which I think is the reason Henczel and McPherson are bothering with him."

"Sounds like you have figured out something," Joe said.

"I looked through the hand bills that have come through," Broddy said, "Neither man is wanted."

"You were expecting them to be?" Joe asked.

"I thought I would check in case," Broddy answered.

"So, you don't like them either?" Joe asked.

"Something about them," Broddy answered, "But I can't exactly pinpoint what it is."

"Henczel thinks they are here to kill Mr. Cheshire," Joe said.

"Not sure that is it," Broddy said, "Somehow they don't seem like killers to me. Maybe thieves."

"I don't think Mr. Cheshire had much to steal," Joe said.

"A pocket watch," Broddy said, "Which someone else feels they owned until he took it back."

"The two men tell the same tale as I heard?" Joe asked.

"What did you hear?" Broddy asked.

"The one man is claimed to be Mr. Cheshire's son," Joe answered.

"Makes sense if he wants the pocket watch," Broddy said, "Then people are much more likely to lead him directly to Mr. Cheshire. People like to help out family."

"Becomes a question about what to do when Mr. Cheshire

146

would have been confused as to who the man is," Joe said, "Not that he currently has much concern about the matter."

"An excuse for his lack of reaction can be thought up," Broddy said, "And if Mr. Cheshire isn't around, they can just claim the pocket watch as a family heirloom. I did talk to Rachelle this afternoon and she has been warned about the men. She isn't going to be giving up anything to them."

"Sounds like everything is fine, except for the matter of the two wandering around," Joe said.

"I'm not sure they are going to wandering much longer with Henczel and McPherson scheming," Broddy said. He had finished his drink and indicated for a refill. Joe refilled it.

"You sure you don't know what they are planning?" Broddy asked.

"And have you charge me with being an accessory?" Joe asked.

"At this point, aside from not knowing the plan, I could be an accessory," Broddy answered.

"I still don't know the plan," Joe answered.

Broddy nodded. He knew Joe was lying but was not going to push the matter right now. After taking a sip of his drink, Broddy turned and checked over the room again. Joe was not bothering to check the room as he was partly busy pouring drinks and also he was not as worried about the matter with Broddy sitting there. Not that he had been worried before Broddy showed up, as most of the people who likely to cause trouble had not come in.

The saloon door swung open. Henczel and McPherson entered. They came over to the bar and took seats.

"A drink for us," Henczel said, "We are thirsty."

Joe poured drinks for Henczel and McPherson only once Henczel had set the money on the bar.

"Where are Justin and his friend this evening?" Joe asked.

"They were talking in the dining room of the Lanaway hotel," Henczel answered, "They might just go to bed rather than come here, but we don't know for sure."

"You talked to them?" Sheriff Broddy asked, "Or you just watching them?"

"Watching them," McPherson answered, "We aren't ready to talk to them yet."

"And when you do talk to them?" Sheriff Broddy asked.

"Justin asked if we could take him to visit Mr. Cheshire," McPherson answered.

"You going to have him dig up a grave?" Sheriff Broddy asked.

"No," McPherson answered, "We have no plans to disturb Mr. Cheshire or anyone else already six feet under."

"That is good to know," Sheriff Broddy said, "But I am still concerned about whatever plan you two have been thinking up."

"We have a plan?" Henczel asked.

"Well, if you are taking them to meet Mr. Cheshire, you are planning something," Sheriff Broddy answered, "And I understand why but I do have to warn you to stay within the law."

"You think we would break the law?" Henczel asked.

"There is a large possibility," Sheriff Broddy answered, "Because Justin is trespassing on an important person in your minds and you don't want him to mess with anything to do with Mr. Cheshire. But if you break the law, I will have to arrest and charge you."

"We are not planning to break the law," McPherson said.

"Good," Sheriff Broddy said, "Because I really don't want to arrest the newspaper editor and the current mayor."

"Does our positions in the community matter that much?" Henczel asked.

"No," Sheriff Broddy answered, "I just don't want to arrest you, especially since I don't think those two are worth it."

McPherson shrugged. Henczel did not really respond. Joe offered to refill Broddy's glass and Broddy nodded. Joe filled

it. He had to move down the bar to fill someone else's glass.
If the conversation continued, he could not hear them. There
were several people who needed serving since he was there.
Finally he moved back but no one was talking at that moment.

Matt raised his voice slightly as he and Michael were
starting into their usual fight. Sheriff Broddy twitched but
otherwise did not move.

"You want me to remove tonight's entertainment?" Sheriff
Broddy asked Joe.

"Not yet," Joe answered, "They can stay until they start
breaking furniture."

"Very well," Sheriff Broddy said.

Before Michael could yell back at Matt, the salon door
swung open. In stepped Justin and his friend. Most of the
people in the saloon were focused on Matt and Michael, but
those close to the door fell quiet at the entrance of Justin and
his friend. It was only as they fell quiet that others started
looking toward the door. When they realized the audience
was paying attention to something else, Matt and Michael
stopped their argument.

"Apparently they aren't staying at the hotel for the evening,"
Sheriff Broddy said under his breath. Neither Henczel nor
McPherson said anything.

DeWhite got to his feet. His movements suggested he
was not happy about the matter. He walked over to the two
men. They had stopped just inside the door and due to the
response of the people they had not moved farther inside.
When DeWhite stopped in front of them, they stared at him
for a moment and he stared back. Then the two men turned
and walked out of the saloon with DeWhite following them.

Sheriff Broddy got to his feet to go after them. Before he
could get very far across the room, there was a loud voice
singing off-key.

"The woman of the east. She awaits the letter. Of her love
who is far away. The man who headed west. To find his fortune

for his love. His fortune in gold."

Suddenly the singing stopped and there were three shots fired. Sheriff Broddy started to run. Joe came out from behind the bar before following the sheriff. Henczel and McPherson were behind them. Some people stayed where they were and others were slowly moving to find out what happened. The sheriff was out the door before Joe even reached it. Henczel held the door for everyone else who stepped out.

Out on the sidewalk, Sheriff Broddy was bending over a prone figure. Two others were seated on the wood. Joe looked at them, but it was hard to see anything in the light coming through from inside the saloon. One was not moving, but the other one seemed to be.

"We need to get Doc McKaig," Henczel said.

"Doc McKaig is busy," Sheriff Broddy said, "There is a new lady out at Laine's place who knows some healing."

"I will go," Henczel said before hurrying off the sidewalk and down the road. He grabbed the reins of a horse tied up at a hitching post in front of the next building. Then he galloped off towards Laine's place.

Joe was now close enough to see it was DeWhite lying on the sidewalk. He had a bullet wound in his stomach and was trying not to move. Sheriff Broddy had his hand over the wound and trying to prevent too much blood loss.

The person who was still moving was Justin's friend while Justin was still. The friend did not seem to be injured. However Justin had a hole in his chest, which had leaked blood but not pumping it out.

"What happened?" the friend asked. His voice was quivering.

"You got too close to the phantom singer," Sheriff Broddy answered, "And he shoots when his identity could be found out."

"Is he still alive?" the friend asked.

Joe put his finger to Justin's throat to try to find a pulse. There was none.

"He is gone," Joe said.

"That is murder," the friend said.

"Are you injured?" Sheriff Broddy asked.

"No, the bullets missed me," the friend answered, "I hit the ground at the first shot. I didn't see the shooter."

"People never do," Sheriff Broddy said, "Can you take over?"

"Yes," Joe said. He moved to kneel next to DeWhite and put his hands over the bullet hole. Sheriff Broddy removed his hands. He stood up.

"Everyone back inside," Sheriff Broddy said to those standing around. Everyone standing on the sidewalk slowly headed back inside.

"Go into the kitchen and ask Miss. Edwards to take over the bar," Joe said to McPherson.

"I will," McPherson said before going back inside.

Sheriff Broddy stepped down to the road and began to look around. He was looking for any sign of the phantom singer.

"He isn't going to find anything," DeWhite said.

"But it is his job to look," Joe said.

"I didn't see anything," DeWhite said, "I was not even looking as my focus was on telling them they were not welcome."

"No one said we were banned from going for a drink," the friend said.

"After the scene last night, you don't think there would be an issue if you came back?" DeWhite asked.

"All we were looking for was a drink," the friend said.

Sheriff Broddy came back on the sidewalk.

"You didn't find anything," DeWhite said.

"No, I didn't," Sheriff Broddy said.

DeWhite was quiet and seemed to be trying to stay

conscious. McPherson came back out of the saloon.

"Everything is fine in there," McPherson said.

"Good," Joe said.

"This the first time the phantom singer hit someone," McPherson said.

"I hope it was an accident," Sheriff Broddy said.

"Justin is still dead," the friend said.

"We know," Sheriff Broddy said.

"You need to find him and charge him," the friend said.

"Since he has been shooting at people for years and no one has figured out who he is, there is only so much I can do unless he turns himself in when he finds out he killed someone," Sheriff Broddy said.

"Why are you not taking this matter seriously?" the friend asked.

"I am," Sheriff Broddy answered, "But I am also a realist. He shot at someone and he not only hit them but someone is dead. I will do what I can."

There was the sound of hoofs coming towards them. Joe looked up and saw Henczel coming back on the horse with a woman behind him. Once they reached the saloon, the woman slid down off the horse. She came up on the sidewalk with a bag in her hand. She had long grey hair pinned up to the back of her head. Her coat was lopsided as if it was pulled on in a hurry.

"Thank you, Tracey," Sheriff Broddy asked.

"I couldn't really turn it down," Tracey answered as she knelt beside DeWhite. Joe moved his hands long enough for her to examine the wound. She cut the material away from it to see better.

"We need to get him off the street so I can get the bullet out," Tracey said.

"You can take him up to my room," Miss Karina said from the doorway into the saloon.

"Can you move on your own?" Sheriff Broddy asked.

"I can try," DeWhite answered. Tracey held a piece of cloth to the wound as DeWhite moved with the help of Joe. Sheriff Broddy took over being a crutch for DeWhite as he moved towards the doors to the saloon with Tracey going along. Joe stayed outside on the sidewalk as they went inside.

"What about Justin?" the friend asked from where he had not moved.

"They will be back to deal with him," Joe answered. He took out his handkerchief to wipe the blood off his hands. The wet blood came off easily but the stuff that had dried was harder to get off. He was going to have to find some water to really get it all off his hands.

"Is he going to be okay?" Henczel asked as he came up on the sidewalk.

"It seems like it," Joe answered, "But Justin is dead."

"Damn," Henczel said looking over at the corpse. He moved closer to peer at Justin.

"You were going to help him," the friend said.

"Yes, we were," Henczel said.

"Now you are going to have to find his father to tell him Justin is dead," the friend said, "And that he was murdered with the town sheriff not taking the matter seriously."

"I am sure Sheriff Broddy is taking this death seriously," Henczel said, "As for telling Mr. Cheshire, I will do it."

"It would soften any blow to hear it from you," Joe said.

"Why?" the friend asked.

"Because I spend the most time talking to him," Henczel answered, "Whenever I can I visit him and we talk over a cup of coffee."

"Then you can take me to him and I can tell him what Justin wanted his father to know," the friend said. He started to get to his feet.

"We can't go now," Henczel said.

"Why not?" the friend asked.

"Because it is the middle of the night," Henczel answered,

"Not to mention I don't know if we will get caught out in the desert during a rain storm."

"His son is dead," the friend said, "This is an important matter."

"He hasn't talked to his son in years," Henczel said, "Why is it so important right now?"

"What is going on?" Sheriff Broddy asked.

"I need him to take me to Mr. Cheshire," the friend answered, "Because we need to tell him about his son's death."

"As I just tried to explain about it being night and the rainy season," Henczel said.

"You will take me to him," the friend said as he reached out and grabbed Henczel by the collar.

"Let go of me," Henczel said as he tried to knock the man's arms away. It did not work.

"Justin is dead," the friend said shaking Henczel, "He never got to deliver the message to his father. We need to deliver the message."

"Not now," Henczel said.

"Let go of him," Sheriff Broddy said.

"This has nothing to do with you," the friend said to the sheriff.

"You have the current town mayor by the collar and are being violent with him," Sheriff Broddy said, "It very much has to do to me."

The friend snarled at the sheriff. Sheriff Broddy grabbed the man's arm. He twisted it so the man had to break his hold on Henczel. Sheriff Broddy pulled the man's arm behind his back. Henczel helped to get the man's other hand off his collar. Sheriff Broddy pulled the man's other arm behind his back. Then Sheriff Broddy handcuffed the man.

"I think you will benefit from a night in a holding cell," Sheriff Broddy said. He took the man away and headed towards the sheriff's office.

"I think we might be in trouble," Henczel said.

"I am questioning a few things," Joe said.

"Like what?" Henczel asked.

"We know Mr. Cheshire doesn't have a son," Joe said, "This man knows Justin isn't Mr. Cheshire's son. So, why is he so set and determined to talk to Mr. Cheshire?"

"It is an interesting question," Henczel said.

"What is he thinking he is going to get from finishing what Justin was attempting?" Joe asked.

"Another good question," Henczel said, "McPherson and I will have to have another conversation on the matter."

"Might want include Broddy this time," Joe said, "Because he already knows you two were up to something and you might need his help against the man."

"I will have to find McPherson first," Henczel said.

"He went inside," Joe said.

"Okay, I will see if I can find him," Henczel said. He headed into the saloon. Joe stood there on the sidewalk with only the corpse who had been Justin for company. He looked out over the street. Something glinted in the light coming from inside the saloon. He could not see exactly what it was. Joe stepped down on to the road. He bent down and picked up the object up. Holding it in the palm of his hand, Joe studied the object. It was a shiny button.

It looked like the one he had found in the Grady house. Joe turned it over in his hand. It definitely looked like the one from the Grady house. Whoever had killed Len had been in town in the last twenty-four hours. They had to have been for it to still be so shiny. But there had been plenty of people through town lately. It seemed impossible to figure out who it was without seeing another button on their clothes.

Joe tried to think of anyone he had seen with a button like that. He remembered Slick and his men having shiny buttons, but they were not quite like this one. Also none of them had been seen in town recently. When he and Sheriff Broddy went to visit Slick, Slick had denied having anything to do with Len's death. The only thing Slick had to do with Len was having an affair with Len's wife. Joe believed that to be true.

So, who else could be the owner of the shiny button? Sheriff Broddy had been out here. DeWhite had not only been out here but also fallen making it easier for something to have fallen off his clothes. But Joe did not remember DeWhite wearing any shiny buttons. Henczel had been out here and in a hurry. McPherson had been out here, but he had never gotten off the sidewalk. Justin and his friend were not around when Len was killed. There were others from inside the saloon who might have lost the button. It also could have been anyone who walked passed.

"What is it?" Sheriff Broddy asked.

"A button," Joe answered.

"Why are you so focused on it?" Sheriff Broddy asked.

"Because I found a similar one in the Grady house when we were looking around after he was found dead," Joe answered.

"I remember," Sheriff Broddy said, "Who lost it?"

"I am not sure," Joe answered, "I am sure I saw someone with such buttons but I can't remember who."

"Hopefully it will come to you," Sheriff Broddy said, "Because we haven't been finding a lot of clues as to who it was. If something doesn't turn up soon, I am not sure it will be solved."

"I will try to remember it," Joe said.

"Come on," Sheriff Broddy said, "Help me get Justin to Doc McKaig's office."

"Where is he?" Joe asked.

They moved toward Justin's body. Sheriff Broddy took Justin's shoulders and Joe took Justin's legs.

"He went off to visit his grandchildren," Sheriff Broddy answered, "He will be back tomorrow."

They stepped off the sidewalk. They headed down the street towards the doctor's office.

"Henczel or McPherson tell you whether their plan is now cancelled due to the death of their victim?" Sheriff Broddy asked.

"Henczel said he needed to talk to McPherson about the scheme," Joe answered, "But it doesn't sound like it is cancelled due to Justin's friend demanding to see Mr. Cheshire."

"I will need to talk to them then," Sheriff Broddy said, "I am not sure messing with the friend is a good idea as he seems to have come unhinged with the death of Justin. Those people tend to be dangerous if tricked about something they deem important."

"I told Henczel I was questioning what the friend was getting from finishing what Justin was trying to do," Joe said.

"It is a valid question," Sheriff Broddy said, "But unless he is willing to tell us what is going on and why, we aren't going to get answers."

"Hopefully he is willing to answer," Joe said, "Because knowing what they are here to do to Mr. Cheshire might change how the situation plays out."

"Well, at the moment I don't really have anything to charge him with," Sheriff Broddy said, "I can't charge him for his behaviour towards Henczel because he had just watched his friend being shot as well as being shot at. He could argue he was not thinking straight."

"Few people would in such situations," Joe said, "But I'm not sure he was as panicky as he would like us to believe."

They reached Doc McKaig's office. Sheriff Broddy put down Justin to open the door. Then Sheriff Broddy picked the body back up and they went inside. They placed Justin on the table where Doc McKaig put corpses to examine them. Then Sheriff Broddy placed a sheet over the body. He left a note for Doc McKaig to explain the situation.

Joe left the doctor's office with Sheriff Broddy following him out and closing the door behind them. They headed back to the saloon. Neither spoke as they walked. The town was quiet, especially after all the activity from earlier. Most of the townspeople were either in bed or headed that direction. Not many windows had lights. The moon was hidden behind clouds.

But there was something in the air. Maybe it was anticipation of rain. Or maybe it was something else. Joe could feel a tingling along his skin as if he could feel something was coming. But he could not pinpoint the exact thoughts which led to that feeling. Joe hoped it was just more rain. Then he could stay in and avoid getting wet. Stay in where it was warm and dry.

"It is going to rain again," Broddy said.

"Certainly feels like it," Joe said.

"I hope it waits until tomorrow at least," Broddy said, "Nothing to hold up Doc McKaig."

"What about burying Justin?" Joe asked.

"I will have to ask his friend whether he wants to take Justin home," Broddy answered, "If not, there is space in the back corner for him. As much as I don't care for digging graves in the rain, whatever it takes not to smell them anymore."

They arrived back at the saloon. Getting up on the sidewalk, the door swung open and Tracey stepped out. Joe and Broddy stopped.

"How is DeWhite?" Sheriff Broddy asked.

"I took the bullet out and sewed up the wound," Tracey answered, "He is going to live but he should keep a look out for infection."

"Thank you for coming in and helping him," Sheriff Broddy said, "The town doctor is out of town today and expected back tomorrow."

"I am glad I could help," Tracey said, "I should get back to Skye."

"I will take you back," Sheriff Broddy said, "Then you

don't have to walk."

"I greatly appreciate it," Tracey said.

Sheriff Broddy and Tracey stepped down off the sidewalk. They headed towards the stable. Joe went into the saloon. Inside there were less people than earlier as they likely finished up their evening and headed home. Those who were left did not bother to look up at Joe. The game had been abandoned with just Shorty seated at the table.

Joe went to the bar and sat down in his usual seat. Miss. Edwards was behind the bar and pouring drinks. She poured him a drink before moving down the bar. McPherson and Henczel moved from where they had been sitting at a table to sit at the bar.

"We expected Sheriff Broddy to come back with you," Henczel said.

"He volunteered to take Tracey back to Laine's Place," Joe said.

"So, we may not be able to talk to him tonight," Henczel said.

"The phantom singer usually doesn't hit the people he shoots at," McPherson said, "And to kill someone is completely new."

"Maybe he was introduced to Justin and his friend and liked them as much as the rest of the town does," Joe said.

"Is there anyone in town who would be willing to kill someone so easily who was not already in the saloon?" Henczel asked.

"The person has to have been willing to kill before this matter," Joe said, "Otherwise he would not be shooting at people to start with."

"There is some truth there," Henczel said, "It just seems strange that anyone in town would be willing to kill so easily and not already be in the saloon for a drink."

"I am sure there must be a few," Joe said.

"But you don't know for certain?" Henczel asked.

"I haven't paid that much attention," Joe answered.

"We thought about changing our plan," McPherson said, "But now we are thinking we just take his friend instead and let Sheriff Broddy in on it."

"You think he will let you murder someone?" Joe asked.

"We aren't going to murder him," McPherson answered, "There is a cave south of here which goes straight through the mountain. It is not impossible to find the way back here but there is another town over there. The hope being that when he reaches the other side, he would realize we tricked him and he would not bother to come back."

"I guess that depends on whether he decides it is worth it to come back and confront you," Joe said.

"That is beside the point right now," McPherson said, "If we aren't setting out to kill him, Sheriff Broddy is much more likely to go along with it. He also wouldn't charge us with murder if there is no murder involved."

"Are you going to give him water before sending him off?" Joe asked.

"Of course," Henczel answered, "Even enough to get to the town on the other side of the mountains. So far the plan isn't to kill him. But should I ever need help planning an actual murder, I know that consulting you on the matter would help me a lot."

"I am not interested in consulting if there is a chance of being arrested as an accomplice," Joe said.

"Sheriff Broddy wouldn't arrest you for that," McPherson said.

"He threatened it when I wouldn't tell him what you two were up to involving Justin," Joe said.

"Not likely to stick though," Henczel said, "We didn't tell you the whole thing and you didn't give us any advice on the matter. You also didn't do anything to help us."

"Which is why he gave up," Joe said.

"You both know it wouldn't work," Henczel said, "Well,

now he will find out straight from us and he can leave you out of it."

"I am fine with being left out of the matter," Joe said.

"You don't feel the need to stop him from doing something against Mr. Cheshire?" McPherson asked.

"Mr. Cheshire is dead," Joe answered, "I don't see it as doing something against Mr. Cheshire. If they tried to get items that belonged to him, it would be against Rachelle and then I may feel the need to do something about them."

"Then we will leave you out of further plans," Henczel said.

"I appreciate that," Joe said.

Henczel and McPherson got up and went back to the table where they were talking before. Joe finished his drink. He pushed the glass over for Miss. Edwards to refill it. She did.

"After this, I will go back to serving people," Joe said to her, "And you can go to bed for the night."

"Take your time," Miss. Edwards said, "It has been a long evening for you."

"Thank you," Joe said.

"Your guest came down to find out what all the fuss was," Miss. Edwards said.

"And?" Joe asked.

"She seemed fairly worried about you," Miss. Edwards answered.

"I am sure she was," Joe said.

"But?" Miss. Edwards asked.

"Conflicted," Joe answered.

"She may disappear if you don't make a case for her to stay," Miss. Edwards said.

"Not sure how I feel on that matter," Joe said, "But if she doesn't want to stay, it is better if I don't try to keep her here."

"Okay," Miss. Edwards said with a shrug. She left him alone to finish his drink.

# Chapter Nine
## Cowhands

Joe came down the stairs to the main room of the saloon to find McPherson talking to two ranch hands, Tyler and Sam. McPherson looked up at Joe.

"Here is one who might be able to answer some questions," McPherson said.

"Depends on your questions," Joe said as he sat down in his usual place.

"You have met Tyler and Sam before, haven't you?" McPherson asked.

"I have," Joe answered, "Though I have not seen them in a while."

"We have been helping out with a couple of cattle drives," Tyler said, "We just got back yesterday. McPherson has been helping us catch up on what has been happening here. But he hasn't been able to answer the questions we came to town to have answered."

"What are the questions?" Joe asked.

"We were looking for work and decided to try Len Grady," Tyler answered, "He is usually willing to give us some work as he really doesn't have anyone else to help out on his ranch."

"He had been part of the same cattle drive as us but he had to leave early," Sam said.

"Why?" McPherson asked.

"Word reached him that the person he left to take care of his cattle wasn't able to keep doing it," Sam answered, "Not to mention some issue with his wife."

"But we couldn't find Len Grady or his wife when we went out to the Grady ranch," Tyler said, "Instead there is a large amount of dried blood on the front porch. We did check on Len's cattle and they seem to be okay, if a few are missing."

"I told them about Sheriff Broddy looking for Mrs. Grady not that long ago," McPherson said, "Then said he had found her but wouldn't say anything else."

"Then why are you not asking Sheriff Broddy what is going on?" Joe asked.

"Because he is busy with some of the matters that came up last night," McPherson answered, "DeWhite showed up at Sheriff Broddy's office this morning about the shooting and Henczel is there to deal with Justin's friend."

"Did Doc McKaig arrive back in town?" Joe asked.

"Yes," McPherson answered, "He arrived this morning. He is in Sheriff Broddy's office as well. I think part of the discussion is what to do with Justin's body."

"Has that matter been settled?" Joe asked.

"I don't think so," McPherson answered, "The big problem being Justin's friend doesn't want to head back to wherever Justin came from until he has gotten to talk to Mr. Cheshire."

"You just told us Mr. Cheshire died," Sam said.

"He did," Joe said, "But then the man named Justin arrived in town and claimed to be Mr. Cheshire's son, which we all know to be a lie. So, McPherson and Henczel were going to get rid of Justin and his friend. Except that Justin is now dead and they don't want to give up the fact that Mr. Cheshire is dead and wouldn't care to be notified about Justin's death if he was alive. Now they are trying to get rid of the friend and the body."

"Sounds pretty complicated," Tyler said, "Does any of this have to anything to do with Len?"

"Not really," Joe answered, "That is a separate matter."

"I figured Sheriff Broddy must have involved you in whatever was going on with Len Grady because you have been going off with him fairly regularly lately," McPherson said.

"As a member of council, Sheriff Broddy felt he needed

my assistant in the matter," Joe said, "So, yes, I do know what is going on. But Sheriff Broddy was not sure he wanted it reported for the town to hear."

"What did happen?" Tyler asked, "We aren't going to tell anyone."

Joe looked at McPherson. Tyler and Sam did the same. They waited. McPherson shifted uncomfortably but did not say anything for a moment.

"Fine," McPherson said, "I will not tell anyone about this matter, but I really should keep to my duty as the newspaper editor."

"But you won't," Tyler said.

"I will not tell anyone," McPherson said.

"Len was found dead on his front porch," Joe said, "His wife couldn't be found anywhere at the ranch or in town. But she was found. Apparently she was at home when Len arrived home a day early and she heard him being murdered, so she took off to protect herself."

"If she wasn't out at the ranch and wasn't in town, where did she go?" McPherson asked, "Where else could she go?"

"She went into hiding with her lover," Joe answered, "Once Sheriff Broddy figured out who that was, it was easy to find her."

"But who killed him?" Tyler asked.

"Sheriff Broddy hasn't figured that out yet," Joe answered, 'He has been working on it since the body was found."

"Was part of the investigation wandering the desert in search of a runaway horse?" McPherson asked.

"Len's horse is missing," Joe answered, "Someone thought they had seen it wandering out in the desert, but it turned out to be wrong."

"Have you figured out what did happen to Len's horse?" McPherson asked.

"No," Joe answered, "We are figuring that whoever killed Len stole his horse. Since we don't know who that is, we don't know where the horse is."

"But if you find the horse, it may lead you to who killed him," Sam said.

"Yes," Joe said.

"We need to find some work, so we can watch for Len's horse while we do so," Tyler said.

"If you do find Len's horse, report it to Sheriff Broddy," Joe said, "He would appreciate the information."

"Mrs. Grady's lover doesn't live in town?" McPherson asked.

"He doesn't," Joe answered.

"Len was right to be worried about his wife cheating on him," Sam said, "There was some on the drive who laughed at the idea she would be with someone else. Except that in investigating the matter, Len went to his death."

"He didn't know," Tyler said.

"None of us ever do," Sam said.

"Sometimes it can be known," Joe said, "It is matter of knowing the situation before walking into it. Len either didn't know or didn't think that his death would be the outcome."

"If you know there was a possibility of your death, would you go into the situation?" Sam asked, "Or would you avoid it?"

"It depends on the situation," Joe answered, "Why am I tempted to walk into the situation? If there is a good reason, I will go into it and hope I will make it through. If the reason is not good enough, I would avoid it. The danger to me has to be worth it."

"That does make sense," Sam said.

"It becomes more of a question what being worth dying over," Tyler said.

"That is a harder question to answer," Joe said, "And it is very much dependant on each person."

"It would take my fiancée being in danger," McPherson said, "Not cheating on me but her in danger."

"Back when I was married, I would have done the same for her," Tyler said.

"But you aren't married now," Sam said.

"I am not," Tyler said, "She granted me a divorce after she had a child by another man. I haven't met anyone since who I would walk into danger for."

"There is no person I would go to my death for," Sam said, "I like my life more than anyone else's."

"Maybe someday you will meet someone who will mean that much to you," Tyler said.

"Maybe," Sam said.

The door to the kitchen opened and Miss. Edwards came out with a plate of food. She set it in front of Joe before going back to the kitchen. Sam leaned over and smelled the food.

"You have to pay her if you want some," Joe said.

"Good idea," Sam said. He got up and headed for the door to the kitchen. Tyler hesitated a moment and then followed him.

"I doubt they have eaten this morning," McPherson said.

"That is fine," Joe said with a shrug, "Miss. Edwards runs the kitchen, so if they are willing to pay her they can ask for food."

"The kitchen is attached to your saloon," McPherson said.

"So?" Joe asked with a shrug.

The door from the kitchen opened and Sam and Tyler came out with their own plates of food. They sat down at the bar again.

"One of the best deals on food," Sam said before he started eating.

McPherson let everyone eat as Tyler and Sam had their sole focus being the food in front and a complete lack of interest in a conversation. Joe took the opportunity to eat as well. When he was finished, so were the other two and Miss. Edwards came out for the plates.

"I suppose it is too much to ask for a drink at this time of day," Tyler said.

"If you have the coins, you can get a drink," Joe said.

Tyler and Sam came up with the coins for the drinks. Joe got up and went behind the bar. He poured the drinks for them.

"Thank you," Tyler said before taking a sip.

"No alcohol on that particular cattle drive," Sam said, "So, this is a good." He took a sip and sighed with pleasure.

"And that is why I run a saloon," Joe said.

"You aren't drinking yet?" McPherson asked.

"I have some things I have to do today before I start drinking," Joe answered.

"Are we taking up your time?" McPherson asked.

"A little bit," Joe answered, "But that is part of running a business." Joe sat back down in his spot.

"We will buy one more drink before we go to justify taking up your time," Tyler said.

"I appreciate it," Joe said.

"What is Sheriff Broddy's next step in the investigation into Len's death?" McPherson asked.

"I don't know," Joe said, "We were focused on other things the last time we talked," Joe answered, "But when he is finished with everyone else, you can ask him."

"He may not want to tell me," McPherson said, "Especially if he didn't want to tell me to start with."

"I can't help you with that," Joe said, "I wasn't supposed to talk to you about it."

"The other drink?" Tyler asked.

Joe got up and went behind the bar again. He poured the drinks for Tyler and Sam. They paid him. Then Joe went back to sit down.

"Hopefully the case can be closed soon," Tyler said, "It is not good to have a murderer wandering around."

"We already have the Phantom Singer," McPherson said.

"The Phantom Singer is harmless," Tyler said, "He shoots at people but he always misses."

"Not the last time," McPherson said, "Yesterday he killed a man and hit DeWhite."

"Why would DeWhite go out when the Phantom Singer is singing?" Sam asked, "We all know not to do that if we don't want to get shot at."

"He was talking to two men," McPherson answered, "The two men looking to talk to Mr. Cheshire. They had gone out to talk before the Phantom Singer started singing and happened to be out there when he started."

"Maybe he didn't like them looking for Mr. Cheshire," Sam said, "Most people around here wouldn't like that."

"The idea has been put out there," Joe said, "But without asking the Phantom Singer, we don't know for sure."

"Sheriff Broddy is probably having to look for him along with whoever killed Len," McPherson said, "He is also trying to help figure out what to do with the two men who came looking for Mr. Cheshire."

"I am sure he will figure it all out," Tyler said, "We will keep our eyes out for Len's horse and help him that way."

"As much as we can," Sam said.

"The rest of us will wait to see what Sheriff Broddy has to say about the two men and the Phantom Singer," Joe said.

"That may take some time," McPherson said.

"I don't know that there is a rush," Joe said, "I mean aside from the body starting to smell."

"Still better to solve the situations sooner," McPherson said.

"We will be back in town to hear about things later," Tyler said, "But we should find some work for today."

Tyler and Sam got up.

"Talk to you later," McPherson said.

"We expect a full update then," Tyler said. Then he and Sam left the saloon.

"When he was done, Henczel said he would meet me here,"

McPherson said.

"I have some work to do," Joe said, "But you can stay around."

"Thank you," McPherson said.

Joe reached under the bar and pulled out his ledger. He opened it to the place marked with a pencil. Leaning over the ledger, Joe started his work. McPherson took out his notebook and started writing in it.

At some point Jake came in and started getting things ready for opening. He and Joe consulted about supplies at times, but otherwise everyone worked on their own. Miss. Edwards came out and talked to Joe about things in the kitchen for a short period. Then she went back to the kitchen.

It was likely an hour or so since Joe got up when Henczel came into the saloon. He sat down next to McPherson. McPherson put away his notebook.

"What happened?" McPherson asked.

"Justin's friend is making demands," Henczel answered, "But Sheriff Broddy isn't letting him have whatever he wants."

"Was any decisions made?" McPherson asked.

"Sheriff Broddy doesn't seem very interested in investigating who the Phantom Singer is," Henczel answered, "Justin's friend is pressing for murder charges against him."

"So, what is going to happen?" McPherson asked.

"Sheriff Broddy has offered Justin's friend a seat on the coach and luggage space for Justin," Henczel answered.

"Is he taking it?" McPherson asked.

"Not without an argument," Henczel answered.

"What is Sheriff Broddy going to do?" McPherson asked.

"There was a suggestion about letting Justin have the seat in the coach and his friend in the luggage space," Henczel answered, "But I don't think the driver would agree to that as dead bodies are not something people want to sit next to."

"What about his demands to see Mr. Cheshire?" McPherson asked.

"He has dropped it," Henczel answered, "I think someone

might have told him the truth, but I am not certain about that."

"Did Sheriff Broddy figure out why Justin and his friend wanted to find Mr. Cheshire?" McPherson asked.

"The man who stole the watch from Mr. Cheshire put money out on getting it back," Henczel answered, "Justin was the man's son, who apparently hoped to inherit the watch and thought it was a family heirloom that was stolen by Mr. Cheshire."

"Well, if he was willing to steal the watch from Mr. Cheshire, he would be willing to lie to his family about it," McPherson said.

The door to the saloon opened and DeWhite limped inside. He nodded towards them before heading upstairs.

"He is still staying here?" Henczel asked.

"Apparently," Joe answered, "Doc McKaig probably told him not to be alone for a few days. Miss. Karina will make sure he isn't alone."

"It doesn't bother you?" Henczel asked.

"She has paid the rent for the month," Joe answered with a shrug, "If he wants to eat, he has to discuss that separately with Miss. Edwards."

"So, what did Justin's friend decide to do?" McPherson asked.

"He is going to take Justin's body back to Justin's father," Henczel answered.

McPherson asked Henczel another question, but Joe tuned it out. His mind was on the pocket watch. Mr. Cheshire had showed it to Joe a few times. He kept it a brightly polished. It reminded Joe of the shiny buttons; the button from the Grady house and the matching one from the street outside the saloon. His mind went over the investigation in search of someone who might have lost the buttons.

When he and Sheriff Broddy went out to Slick's hideout, Joe had noticed Slick and some of his men wearing bright buttons. It was used as decoration on their pants and coats. But those buttons did not match the ones Joe found. The buttons from Slick and his men were plain and the ones Joe found had a design on them.

There was a flash of something shining in the light as Joe shoved the man out of the light and into the darkness. The buttons had come off the sleeve of his coat. It flashed as he had refilled his glass from the bottle on the table. Those buttons did match the two found. And it made sense that he would be the murderer.

He had reported the crime, but there was also a history between him and Len. The fact that Len's horse was missing should have been a very large clue. However, somehow it escaped Joe and Sheriff Broddy. The most obvious clues were the ones they did not see, otherwise Sheriff Broddy would have already made an arrest for Len's death.

Joe thought about getting up and heading out to report his figuring to Sheriff Broddy, but he did not want to leave with McPherson and Henczel sitting in the saloon. It was not like it would matter much whether he reported it to Sheriff Broddy now or in a few hours. Sheriff Broddy was probably still busy with Justin's friend.

"Well?" Henczel's voice interrupted Joe's thoughts.

"What?" Joe asked.

"You weren't listening, were you?" Henczel asked.

"No, my thoughts have been on other matters," Joe answered, "What was the question?"

"Len Grady's murder," Henczel said, "Apparently McPherson found out."

"Yeah, Tyler and Sam reported a blood stain at the Grady place," Joe said.

"We were asking if you had a guess as to who did it," McPherson said.

"Anders," Joe said.

"Why?" McPherson asked.

"Len's horse is missing," Joe answered, "And the two have had problems with each other for years. Tyler and Sam said more cattle were missing from Len's herd."

"Makes sense," Henczel said.

"Have you talked it over with Sheriff Broddy?" McPherson asked.

"No," Joe answered, "Not yet, but I am sure we will have the discussion later today. I am sure he is busy right now."

"If DeWhite have left him alone and Justin's friend has been dealt with, he likely has the time," Henczel said.

"I still have some work to do," Joe said, "I might as well get that done before I move on to the next thing."

"Okay," Henczel said. He and McPherson went back to their conversation. Joe ignored it and went back to his ledger. Jake had finished most of his work and had left the saloon. He told Joe he would be back before opening. Joe nodded but did not look up.

Finally Joe was finished his work with the ledger. He stuck the pencil into the page as a marker. He tucked the ledger under the bar. Joe decided he was ready for a drink and then he would think about wandering over to talk to Sheriff Broddy's office. He set a glass on the bar.

There was a scream from the kitchen, but it was cut off. Joe was on his feet and ran to see what happened. Pushing the door open, Joe saw Miss. Edwards lying on the floor. Her eyes were closed and she was not moving. Joe went to her side. He was relieved to find she was still alive. On the floor was a pot which was likely used to knock her out.

There was a bang from behind Joe. He turned to look but it was only the back door swinging in the wind. Joe went to the doorway but whoever had left by it was out of sight.

"What happened?" McPherson asked.

"I don't know," Joe answered, "But it seems someone knocked out Miss. Edwards. I didn't see who it was."

Henczel went to the door and outside. Joe went to Miss.

Edwards and gently picked her up.

"Please open the door," Joe asked McPherson and nodded towards a door to one side. McPherson looked in surprise at the door before going and opening it. Inside was a small bedroom. It was barely big enough for the bed and dresser. The ceiling sloped to show it was a room under the stairs. Joe ducked a little to avoid hitting his head while he took Miss. Edwards to the bed and set her down on it.

Joe left the door open after he stepped out of the room. Henczel stepped back inside.

"See anyone?" Joe asked.

"No," Henczel answered, "There was a rider heading down the street but I couldn't see him well enough to identify him."

There was the sound of more people coming to the door of the kitchen. Several of the ladies from upstairs came into sight.

"Oh no," Miss. Karina said, "Is Miss. Edwards okay?"

"We will know when she wakes up," Joe answered, "What happened?"

"Anders," Miss. Karina answered, "I saw him upstairs."

"What was he doing?" Joe asked.

"He was bothering the lady you are letting stay here," Miss. Karina said.

"Scarlett," Zoe said.

"Bothering her how?" Joe asked.

"He took Scarlett with him," Zoe answered.

"Are you sure?" Joe asked.

"Pretty sure," Zoe answered.

There was a groan from the bedroom. Joe went back to the doorway. Miss. Edwards was waking up.

"What happened?" Joe asked.

"Anders was dragging Scarlett out of here," Miss. Edwards answered, "I tried to stop him but I couldn't."

"Are you okay?" Joe asked.

"I have a headache, but otherwise I seem to be fine," Miss.

Edwards answered.

"Good," Joe said. He turned back to the kitchen. McPherson was gone. Miss. Karina went to see how Miss. Edwards was doing.

Joe left the kitchen. He went upstairs long enough to grab his hat and jacket. Then he headed out of the saloon.

Sheriff Broddy stood at the window and stared out. The coffee cup in his hand provided warmth, which he had been seeking out since spent too much time in the rain. Miss. Modahl's soup had helped a lot, but Broddy still found himself feeling cold at odd times. Today was one of those odd times.

It had been a long morning with talking to DeWhite, Henczel, and the man calling himself Levi. Doc McKaig had been helpful in the offering to bury the man named Justin or putting him in a box to ship. Broddy figured the best way to get rid of both Justin and Levi was to send them off on the next stage with only Levi arguing against it. Even with the deputy telling him that Mr. Cheshire was dead, Levi was not willing to let the matter drop.

Broddy would have told them that Mr. Cheshire was dead the night they arrived. It would have saved a lot of difficulty, but he did not know they were looking for Mr. Cheshire when he talked to them the first time. Of course, if they had been upfront about their visit then, there would have been no problem. They would have not been outside when the Phantom Singer started singing last night and no one would have been hurt. Because now if Broddy found out who the Phantom Singer was, he was going to have to arrest the man and charge him.

There was already a murder on Broddy's mind; a murder without a solution. The answer to a dead rancher found with his own knife in his chest. The rancher with a missing horse. A missing horse. Broddy's mind clicked with that last piece moving into place. The missing horse made sense if that was the case as did the argument where Len Grady would be close enough to let the person grab his knife.

The door to the office opened and McPherson burst in.

## Chapter Ten
## The Murderer

Joe stepped out of his saloon. The rain was coming down in sheets. The water was running down the road in streams. Joe would have preferred to go back inside and stay dry, but he could not leave Scarlett at the hands of Anders. Joe stepped down off the sidewalk. He was careful to avoid the deeper streams as he did not want to lose his footing. Joe ran towards the stables.

William was nowhere to be seen. Joe went to the stall where his horse was. He saddled Journey with speed of experience. Leading Journey out to the door of the stable, Joe found Sheriff Broddy outside sitting on his horse.

"McPherson told me what happened," Sheriff Broddy said.

"That was fast," Joe said as he mounted.

"It doesn't take me long to saddle my horse," Sheriff Broddy said, "You think Anders took her to his ranch." They directed their horses out of town and started out at a trot.

"That was where I was heading," Joe said.

They rode without speaking. The road was a mess preventing them from going as fast as Joe would have liked to. The horses tried trotting but occasionally would skitter and slide. Joe cursed under his breath every time because it slowed them down. But with the amount of rain they were lucky to make any progress. The rain made it hard to see much in front of them. Each side of the road were rivers running along the dips there, which was how Joe and Sheriff Broddy knew they were still going along the road.

"This is not good," Sheriff Broddy said.

Joe spit out some of the rain that had ended up in his

mouth but otherwise did not answer. Anders's ranch was further out than the Grady ranch, so it was going to take much longer than Joe wanted to get there.

A loud noise reached Joe. Something up ahead was wrong. Sheriff Broddy must have heard it as well because he and Joe exchanged glances. They kept going because there was nothing to do except go on to see what it was. Joe peered ahead in an attempt to see it before they rode into it. As they moved closer, the rumbling was louder.

Just as it came into view, Joe realized what the noise was. The road ahead was washed out. The river was over six feet across and looked deep. The horses stopped at the edge of the water. Joe urged his horse forward, but Journey was skittish. Sheriff Broddy urged his own horse forward and the horse did. Sheriff Broddy's horse skidded sideways as the water pushed him but the horse was able to stay on its feet. Joe kicked Journey to move forward. This time Journey did. The current in the water pushed him sideways the same as Sheriff Broddy's horse but Journey was able to move forward to the other side of the road.

The water stretched a lot farther than it had first appeared and was more like ten feet. The water came up to the horses' knees. At one point Journey stumbled and Joe had to hold on tight. He was not sure he was going to manage to stay on or that Journey would stay on his feet. But they made it to the other side. Joe stopped Journey to rest and because Sheriff Broddy was not there yet. Joe looked back at the river that used to be a road. Sheriff Broddy and his horse were much farther sideways than Joe had ended up. He was working his way through the water and was being pushed down river.

Joe tried to think of any way to help Sheriff Broddy, but he did not have any supplies that would be of use. Then he tried looking around. There was nothing around, except a fence. Joe went over to the fence. He dismounted before tying the reins to the fence post. Joe pushed on the board. It did not move. He picked at the piece closest to the fence post. It came apart from the fence post. Joe managed to twist it off from there. He took the long board and went back to the edge of the river.

He laid the board out toward where Sheriff Broddy was still fighting the water. Joe set it down in the water and held on as tightly as he could. Sheriff Broddy's horse was able to use the board to work its way out of the middle of the river. Finally the horse reached shallower water and was able to come straight to the edge. Joe let go of the board once the horse was safe. The board was gone in seconds.

"Thank you," Sheriff Broddy said. He spat out some of the water that was in his mouth.

Joe nodded. He headed back to Journey and remounted. They headed along the road again. Joe wanted to speed up to make up for the time lost on the washed out area of the road but there was still streams of water along the road keeping the horses to a slower pace.

In far longer time than Joe really wanted, Anders's ranch came into view between the sheets of rain. Joe and Sheriff Broddy reached the porch. They dismounted and tied their horses to the hitching post out front. Joe followed Sheriff Broddy up on to the porch. There were no lights on in the house. Sheriff Broddy knocked on the door. There was no answer. Sheriff Broddy tried to open the door. It was not locked and Joe followed Sheriff Broddy inside. It was quiet and smelled slightly musty.

"Anders?" Sheriff Broddy called out. There was no answer. Sheriff Broddy went one way and Joe went the other. The house had a front room, which is the direction Joe ended up going into. There were some pieces of homemade furniture and it was lightly decorated. It looked like a woman had once lived there, but Joe had never heard of Anders being married. The front room also looked like no one had used it in a long while.

Joe started towards the door that likely led to the kitchen.

Before he reached it, Joe saw a picture in the dim light coming in from the window. It was a wedding picture. Joe stepped closer to see it better. The man in the picture looked like a young version of Anders. The woman was young and sweet looking, but Joe did not recognize her.

Joe moved on to the kitchen. It was a mess. There were dirty dishes on the table and the floor had not been cleaned in far too long. The window had too much crud on it to see out of. It made the room much darker than the front room. The back door was closed. There was a door to the next room that was also closed. Before Joe could go and open it, it opened and Sheriff Broddy stepped into the kitchen.

"Anything?" Sheriff Broddy asked.

"No one seems to be here," Joe answered, "Did you find anything?"

"No," Sheriff Broddy said, "The bed has been slept in at some point but it is sort of like this kitchen. It has been used but hard to tell when. He must be out in the barn."

"Let's go," Joe said. He moved toward the back door. Sheriff Broddy followed him, They stepped outside and closed the door behind them. It was impossible to see the barn from where they were.

"That way," Sheriff Broddy said pointing out to the field.

"How can you tell?" Joe asked as they started moving forward.

"Because I have been here before," Sheriff Broddy answered, "Every time someone comes to me with reports of missing cattle."

"I guess that makes sense," Joe said.

The ground was muddy and any place there was a dip it was filled with water. They were having to watch the ground to avoid stumbling but also needed to keep an eye on where they were going. It was a while before Joe could actually see the barn.

"Was Anders ever married?" Joe asked.

"A long time ago," Sheriff Broddy answered, "Why?"

"There was a wedding picture in the front room," Joe answered, "But I don't remember ever hearing about him being married."

"Back when it was first suspected he was stealing cattle, her mother packed her up and left with her," Sheriff Broddy said, "As far as I know no one has heard from her or her family since."

"And he didn't go after her?" Joe asked, "Anders seems like someone who would not let his wife go so easily."

"He was sitting in jail when they left," Sheriff Broddy answered, "And for a couple weeks after that. By the time he got out they were long gone."

"Intentionally?" Joe asked.

"No," Sheriff Broddy answered, "That was just how things worked out."

Joe stopped because there was a ditch in the middle of the field and it has filled in with water. Sheriff Broddy did the same. It was not wide, but it looked deep.

"Jump or wade?" Sheriff Broddy asked.

"Might be better to jump," Joe answered, "I don't really want to get soaked in there."

"We can't really get any wetter," Sheriff Broddy said.

Joe gave himself some space to get a run up. At the edge of the ditch he jumped. His one foot landed safely on the other side but the other did not quite. He scrambled quickly to get the other foot up. Joe ended up pull himself up, but he was kneeling in the mud. After he caught his breath, Joe got to his feet and turned back to Sheriff Broddy.

Sheriff Broddy backed up and did the run up before jumping. He landed on the other side but in some mud. He slid and found himself on his back.

"You okay?" Joe asked as he offered Sheriff Broddy a hand up.

"I think so," Sheriff Broddy answered as he let Joe help

him up.

"Why would someone have a ditch like that on their property?" Joe asked as they started moving towards the barn again.

"To slow down anyone coming after him," Sheriff Broddy answered, "He dug it a few years ago."

"He is paranoid about people coming after him," Joe said, "On the other hand, he knows who he had stolen from and whether they would be upset with him."

"No one is town would come out here to kill him," Sheriff Broddy said, "Most of it is his paranoia."

The barn got closer. The ground got muddier and there was less grass to hold the water. Joe could feel himself sliding and he worked to keep himself on his feet. Sheriff Broddy was also having some difficulty staying up. As they worked their way to the barn door, the mud clung to their boots making their feet heavy. It was a breath of relief when they reached the door. Joe pulled the door open and then followed Sheriff Broddy inside. He closed the door behind them. They stood there and listened. All they could hear were the movements and breathing of the animals along with the sounds of the rain outside.

"Anders?" Sheriff Broddy called out. They waited for a response, whether it was voice or movement. There was nothing.

"What other buildings are there on this property?" Joe asked.

"There is a small hut farther out in the fields," Sheriff Broddy answered, "There is a door on the other side of the barn."

They moved forward into the building. The first few stalls had horses. Sheriff Broddy stopped at the last stall with horses.

"What is it?" Joe asked stopping as well.

"That is Len Grady's horse," Sheriff Broddy answered.

"Then we have found his killer," Joe said.

"Not yet we haven't," Sheriff Broddy said, "We just know who did it. We still have to catch him."

"Didn't you tell me that Anders reported to you that Grady was dead?" Joe asked.

"He did," Sheriff Broddy answered.

"He must have done that so you wouldn't suspect him of doing the killing," Joe said, "Because otherwise you would have gone looking for him because some cattle were missing as well has him being dead."

"I don't remember cattle being missing," Sheriff Broddy said.

"The ranch hands Tyler and Sam said some cattle was missing when they told McPherson that there was a blood stain out at Grady's house," Joe said.

"They were most likely to know," Sheriff Broddy said, "Anders probably has been taking one or two at time and working to take the whole herd."

"Well, let's go get him," Joe said.

Sheriff Broddy started moving again. Joe went with him as they headed for the door on the other side of the barn. They did not see anything else that caught their attention. Reaching the other door, Sheriff Broddy pushed it opened. With a sigh, Joe stepped out into the rain. There was a squish of mud under his foot.

Sheriff Broddy led the way across another area lacking grass to the field. Because he did not know where to go, Joe followed along. He slid sideways due to the mud but he managed to catch himself before he fell. Just before they reached the grass, there was a small stream. Joe tried to step over it. His feet slipped and instead of avoiding the mud, Joe fell into it.

Joe struggled to get up. The mud stuck to him making it harder to get up. He could feel his clothes soaking up the dirty water. Only the thought of his reasons for being here kept Joe from giving up and heading back. Sheriff Broddy offered a hand out. Joe took it. Sheriff Broddy pulled him out and on to the grass, where Joe was able to get to his feet. Once he was upright, Joe brushed the worse of the mud off. Then they started across the field.

Joe was starting to feel the amount of physical activity he had put into the journey this far when the hut Sheriff Broddy talked about was visible through the rain. But he kept moving. Sheriff Broddy was only slowing down due to the mount of mud sticking to him.

The hut was half-buried so the roof was the main part of it that was visible. Sheriff Broddy slid down the mud to the door of the hut. There was a puddle at the bottom, but it was not very deep. Joe followed Sheriff Broddy only once Broddy was at the door and still upright. As soon as Joe had joined him, Sheriff Broddy knocked on the door.

"Anders!" Sheriff Broddy called, "It is Sheriff Broddy to talk to you."

"Go away!" Anders called back.

"I can't," Sheriff Broddy said, "I am going to open the door."

"I will blast you away," Anders said.

Joe moved to one side of the door while Sheriff Broddy moved to the other. Sheriff Broddy pushed the door open. There was no blast from inside as the door moved inward. Sheriff Broddy peeked around the doorway. Then there was the blast of a shotgun. A pellet went through the wood beside Joe's head but otherwise he was not hit. Joe quickly ducked down and ended squatting in the puddle with his arms over his head. Sheriff Broddy had ducked down as well. He took out his gun once he was down there.

"I'll go first," Sheriff Broddy said. It was quiet enough for Joe to hear him but Anders could not.

"Go ahead," Joe said. Sheriff Broddy peeked around the doorway again. There was no blast this time. Joe peeked into the hut. Anders was standing there with the shotgun at ready. Behind him was Scarlett. She was hogtied and gagged, but otherwise appeared unharmed. The only furniture in the hut was a table and chair. It was to one side. Sheriff Broddy stood up and got ready.

"You have kidnapped the lady," Sheriff Broddy said, "We need to talk about that."

"No, we don't," Anders said. Joe could hear Anders preparing to shoot again. Sheriff Broddy must have heard it too because he ducked down again. The blast went through the wall above where Sheriff Broddy was. Part of the wall disappeared in the blast.

"I told you to go away," Anders said. He was reloading the shotgun. Sheriff Broddy stayed low as he entered the hut. Anders tried to hurry as he reloaded. Sheriff Broddy slammed into him knocking the shotgun away. He knocked Anders to the dirt floor. Joe followed Sheriff Broddy into the hut. He went toward Scarlett. She made a noise of happiness at the sight of him.

Anders knocked the gun out of Sheriff Broddy's hand and it went across the hut from where they were. Sheriff Broddy punched Anders. Anders put up his arm to block the punch. They rolled around as they hit each other against the floor. Sheriff Broddy lost his hat and they rolled over it.

Joe took out his knife. He used it to cut the rope holding Scarlett. He removed the gag first before moving to cut the rope around her wrists.

"Thank you for coming," Scarlett said, "I was scared no one realized I was missing."

"Someone did," Joe said. The knife went through the rope and Scarlett was able to free her hands. Joe moved on to the next rope holding her. He quickly got through that. Once her arms were free, Scarlett hugged Joe. Then he was able to get back to cutting the ropes holding her.

Sheriff Broddy and Anders grunted as they fought. They

rolled close to the wall and Sheriff Broddy hit Anders into the wood. This caused Anders to loosen his grip enough for Sheriff Broddy to get free. Sheriff Broddy got up and used his shoulder to smack Anders into the wall again. Anders slumped down. Sheriff Broddy got to his knees. He reached over and picked up his hat. Sheriff Broddy hit it on his thigh to knock the dust off and then put it back on. Then he started to get to his feet.

Before Sheriff Broddy could finish getting up, Anders tackled him and knocked him back to the floor. Sheriff Broddy's hat fell back into the dirt. He tried to hit Anders but missed. Anders grabbed the side of Sheriff Broddy's head and smacked it into the floor. Sheriff Broddy tried to push back. Anders hit Sheriff Broddy's head into the dirt again. This time Sheriff Broddy went limp and then did not move.

Joe had gotten Scarlett free. She was working to get to her feet as she worked to get the circulation back in her arms and legs. Joe put his knife away. The gasp from Scarlett let Joe know there was a big problem with Sheriff Broddy and Anders. He turned to look. Anders was scrambling off Sheriff Broddy and towards where Sheriff Broddy's gun was lying.

Joe reached out and grabbed the shotgun from the floor beside. He brought it with him as he stood up and turned to Anders. Once he had the gun in his hand, Anders turned to Joe. He laughed at seeing the gun pointed toward him.

"You will never shoot me," Anders said.

"Why not?" Joe asked, "What is going to stop me? You?"

"You don't even own one," Anders said, "Otherwise you would have used it to get rid of people from your saloon."

"Like you?" Joe asked, "Because I never needed a gun to get you out of my saloon. You would have been a waste of bullets."

Anger flared in Anders eyes and he brought the gun up ready to fire. Before he could pull the trigger, Joe did. The shotgun blasted. Pellets peppered Anders causing him to drop the gun. He collapsed to the floor. Joe went over to Anders. He kicked the gun away before pointing the shotgun at Anders. The shotgun was steady in his hands.

"Give me a reason to remove you from this life," Joe said. Anders lay there staring up at the shotgun. The anger was still there and he lifted his head. His mouth opened to say something. Joe pulled the trigger. Blood splattered the wall as well as Joe's clothing. Anders fell back and did not move.

"I figured these clothes were beyond saving anyway," Joe said to himself.

There was a groan from Sheriff Broddy. Joe put the shotgun down beside Anders's body. Then he went over to Sheriff Broddy. Sheriff Broddy was slow to sit up.

"I'm going to have a headache," Sheriff Broddy said, "Anders?"

"Is no longer an issue," Joe answered.

"Good," Sheriff Broddy said, "I trust it was self-defence."

"Him or me," Joe said.

"Okay," Sheriff Broddy said. Joe offered his hand to Sheriff Broddy. Sheriff Broddy took the hand and let himself be helped to his feet. He went over and picked up his gun. Then he went and got his hat. Once again, he knocked the dust off before putting it on. It was still very dirty as the dirt was sticking to the water. His soaking clothing was covered with the dust from the floor from the hut. He was moving without showing signs of injury.

"Now we need to head back," Sheriff Broddy said.

"I'm ready when you are," Joe said. They looked at Scarlett.

"The sooner we leave the better," Scarlett said.

"You might think differently once we are out in the rain," Joe said.

"Better in the rain than with him," Scarlett said as she glanced at what was left of Anders.

Sheriff Broddy went out the door with Joe and Scarlett

following him into the rain and the mud.

Joe felt tired but warm as he went down the stairs to the main room of his saloon. The mud was gone and he was dry. His muscles complained about any and all movements. However, he did not feel like sitting in his room by the fire by himself. Jake was behind the bar serving the drinks as he was supposed to be.

Joe sat down in his usual spot. Jake poured him a drink. Joe took a long drink and enjoyed the warmth of it going down his throat. He closed his eyes to feel more of that sensation.

"Did you find her?" McPherson's voice came from nearby.

"Yes," Joe answered. He opened his eyes and McPherson had sat down at the bar.

"Sheriff Broddy arrested Anders for kidnapping?" McPherson asked.

"He said something about waiting until after the rain was over before sending the deputy for the body," Joe answered.

"I guess that happens," McPherson said.

"It does," Joe said. He took another drink and closed his eyes to let the welcomed sensations pass through him.

"Did he hurt her?" McPherson asked.

"She did not seem to be injured," Joe answered, "A little cold and wet by the time we got back. Scared during the ordeal. Probably a little more scared on the way back."

"Why?" McPherson asked.

"Because Sheriff Broddy and I found Len Grady's horse in Anders's barn," Joe answered.

"Anders killed Grady?" McPherson asked.

"It appears that way," Joe answered, "Grady probably accused Anders of stealing his cattle and angered Anders."

"There was likely to be more than some truth to Anders stealing Grady's cattle," McPherson said, "He had been accused of stealing cattle from other people."

"I didn't know much about Anders," Joe said, "He just came in occasionally to get drunk and spend time with a lady upstairs. Half the time he was much too rude for the lady to want to service him and I ended up kicking him out."

"Probably all you wanted to know about him," McPherson said, "He was not someone most of us wanted to spent time with."

"I didn't know he was married," Joe said.

"That was the reason he paid for a woman," McPherson said, "He couldn't remarry because he was never granted a divorce."

"Probably would have had to buy another wife," Joe said.

"That was how he got the first one," McPherson said, "He paid her family for her hand in marriage. I doubt anyone would mourn him."

"I am going to leave it all up to Sheriff Broddy to figure out what to do with Anders and his ranch," Joe said, "I think I have earned the right to go back to minding my own business."

"What about Scarlett?" McPherson asked.

"What about her?" Joe asked.

"You went out into a storm to save her," McPherson answered.

"I couldn't leave her with Anders," Joe said, "No one deserves to be left to that fate."

"So, she is going to stick around?" McPherson asked.

"I don't know what she is going to do," Joe answered, "I didn't ask her."

"Will you?" McPherson asked.

"Why?" Joe asked.

"Will you ask her to stay?" McPherson asked.

"I don't see any reason to do that," Joe answered, "It is better to let her make her own decisions about coming and going."

"But you could ask her to stay," McPherson said, "If she

was around you wouldn't be alone so much."

"I can spend plenty of time alone without being lonely," Joe said, "As I don't feel lonely, I don't see the need to ask something of someone that they might not be able to do. Investing in Scarlett might not be the best for me."

"But…" McPherson said but stretched the word out.

"If she decides to stay that is up to her," Joe said with a shrug.

McPherson smiled but did not say anything. His smiled suggested he was hearing things Joe was not saying.

"Don't," Joe said.

"Don't what?" McPherson asked.

"I will kick you out of my saloon," Joe answered.

"I am not doing anything," McPherson said.

Joe moved his glass towards Jake for a refill. Jake did and moved it back to Joe's hand. Joe picked up the glass and drained it in one gulp. It felt good in his throat. The warmth was starting in his stomach and working its way up through his chest. He put the glass where it could be refilled. Jake did.

"You are going to get drunk," McPherson said.

"Why are you worried about it?" Joe asked.

"Because I don't want to you to drink the town dry," McPherson answered, "If you drink it all, there won't be any for the rest of us."

"You don't look like you are missing much for alcohol," Joe said.

"You aren't even looking at me," McPherson said.

"I can smell it on your breath," Joe said, "I don't need to see your face."

"DeWhite went home earlier," McPherson said, "He left while you were out saving Scarlett."

"Good to know he is still alive," Joe said.

"He said he would be back at the game tomorrow," McPherson said.

"I am sure someone will be happy to hear the game is

going to happen," Joe said, "And it means I don't have to find someone else to run the game."

"I wonder if Sheriff Broddy will ever find the Phantom Singer," McPherson said.

"I don't know," Joe said, "As I already said I am no longer minding other people's business."

"You don't consider the Phantom Singer your business?" McPherson said.

"His identity isn't," Joe said.

"But someday you might be out there accidentally and he will shoot at you," McPherson said.

"It is possible," Joe said, "Still doesn't make it my business. It might be yours, but you are the newspaper editor and need something to put in your paper."

"You could tell me stories," McPherson said, "Then it would be a long while before I would have to go searching for a story."

"That will not be happening anytime soon," Joe said.

"Maybe another drink?" McPherson asked.

"It would take more than that," Joe answered. Joe moved his empty glass toward Jake, who refilled it. Joe took the glass back.

"But you can pay for as many drinks as you want," Joe said.

"If you are going to drink the town dry, I can't afford the bill," McPherson said.

"Then you aren`t going to get any stories for your newspaper," Joe said.

"That is a high price to pay," McPherson said, "But someday I will get some stories from you."

"Sheriff Broddy has a similar goal," Joe said, "Not sure either of you will win."

"We'll see," McPherson said. Joe heard him get up and leave.

A moment went by and then Joe heard someone else sit down. Joe opened his eyes to see who it was. Scarlett was the one sitting there. Despite it being pulled back, Joe could tell her hair was still wet from the bath. It was a slightly fancier dress than her usual wear. This evening her lips matched her name.

"I wanted to thank you again," Scarlett said.

"It isn't a problem," Joe said.

"Maybe I am wrong but it seems to be that you don't put your neck out for many people," Scarlett said.

"I don't do it often," Joe said.

"Then I definitely need to thank you for saving me," Scarlett said.

"You are welcome," Joe said.

"I want to thank you," Scarlett said. She stretched out and put her hand on his. He did let it sit there.

"Of course," Joe said. He finished his drink before taking her hand in his. They got up. She took the lead as they went up the stairs. When they reached her room, Scarlett opened the door and led him inside. Joe closed the door behind them.

Broddy had changed clothing and dried off before going back to his office. He was sitting at his desk when his deputy arrived. The deputy shook off some of the water from his coat before removing it.

"What happened?" the deputy asked as he got himself a cup of the coffee, "When I arrived you were gone."

"I went out to Anders' ranch to help McGraw rescue Scarlett," Sheriff Broddy answered.

"Were you successful?" the deputy asked.

"Yes and no," Sheriff Broddy answered, "Anders was not arrested, but the lady was rescued. I also found evidence that Anders killed Len Grady and stole his horse. You can go out and get Anders once the rain has stopped. Though I suggest you be careful when you go as the road was washed out in places along the way."

"Very well," the deputy said.

"I doubt there will be much excitement this evening," Broddy said, "Levi is still in the cell, DeWhite is resting from his gunshot wound, and all other trouble-makers aren't likely to go out into that rain."

"What about McGraw?" the deputy asked.

"If he isn't busy tonight, I would question a few things in this life," Broddy answered, "Scarlett is going to keep him busy. After the events of today, I think I will leave you to keep the peace for tonight."

Broddy got up and put on his own coat. He headed out the back door to his own place, which was not far. He could not wait to get into his own bed and get a sound sleep.

Joe was sitting in his spot having breakfast when Sheriff Broddy stepped inside the saloon with another man. The other man was in a black suit and wore a silver marshal's badge on his chest. They came over to where Joe was sitting.

"I am here looking for this woman," the marshal asked as he showed Joe a picture. It was a picture of Scarlett.

"She is staying in the second room at the top of the staircase," Joe answered.

"Thank you," the marshal said with a nod.

He headed up the stairs. Sheriff Broddy did not follow the marshal. Instead he sat down at the bar.

"Quiet morning?" Sheriff Broddy asked.

"So far," Joe answered, "Not really expecting much for excitement today. Unless you have brought some with you."

"Not today," Sheriff Broddy said, "The marshal showed up this morning with the hand bill. That was the most excitement of my day."

"Has it dried out enough to dig the grave?" Joe asked.

"Not really," Sheriff Broddy answered, "I don't really expect it to until tomorrow at least. Mrs. Grady sent a message that she will come back into town tomorrow. So Len Grady's estate will all be dealt with then."

"Sounds like everything has been wrapped up with the case," Joe said.

"I had to hire Tyler and Sam to take care of Anders cattle until it can be figured out what to do with them," Sheriff Broddy said, "But otherwise, yes."

"A few people might want to reclaim their cattle from him," Joe said.

"I expect that," Sheriff Broddy said.

"McPherson was asking yesterday about the Phantom Singer," Joe said.

"I figured he would," Sheriff Broddy said, "But I expected him to ask me, not you."

"He figured that since I was helping you with investigating Grady's death, I might know more about your investigation into the Phantom Singer," Joe said, "And it happened outside my saloon."

"But it happened outside," Sheriff Broddy said, "Not inside."

"Even if it happened inside, it is your investigation," Joe said.

"I'm still working on it," Sheriff Broddy said, "With Justin's friend gone and DeWhite not interested in me looking into the case, there isn't much of a rush."

"DeWhite isn't interested in you investigating?" Joe asked, "Sounds suspicious."

"I thought so too," Sheriff Broddy said.

The marshal came down the stairs with Scarlett. She was handcuffed and he had one hand on her arm and her bag in his other hand. He walked her passed them. She looked at Joe with eyes asking for him to stop this. Scarlett was not fighting the marshal but if Joe made any signal that he would help her, she would have done it. Joe picked up his glass and took a sip. He gave no sign of seeing the look. The marshal took Scarlett out of the saloon.

"You knew," Sheriff Broddy said.

"It takes one to know one," Joe said.

"So, will you name come up on a hand bill?" Sheriff Broddy asked.

"I did my time," Joe answered.

# ABOUT THE AUTHOR

Heather Mantler is a lover of fairy tales and fables. Her home town is Prince George, British Columbia. Heather is always working on another story as she hopes to finish every story idea that she has ever written down. She was a nominee for the fiction category of the 2012 Prince George Regional Arts and Cultural Awards and short listed for the 2013 John Harris Fiction Awards. Her blog is heathersdomain.wordpress. com. Heather encourages her readers to post reviews on Good Reads and Amazon.

Books by B. Heather Mantler
Committed to Her Enemy
Chenarcor: Adventures of Alex & Toby
Princess or Pirate
A Thief in Search of a Baby
The Best Brownie Recipe
An Adventure for Princess Aurelia
The Prince and the Mermaid

Kings of Proster Books
For Wealth and Glory
Closing the Portal
Mistakes Made
Wasted Love
The Mystery of the Magic
Lovers & Losses
Fighting for the King
The King's Ransom